Praise for *Common People*

'Birch throws us straight into the action. There is always urgency and vitality in his stories; there is always a wide terrain. Characters are immediately and completely drawn with just a few words, and do not fit into easily defined moulds.'

—*Weekend Australian*

'The stories are varied, sustained and filled with beautiful writing that shows a rare talent for getting inside the minds of a huge cast of characters. There is not one word out of place.'

—*The Herald Sun*

'*Common People* is a book of great empathy and even greater faith.'

—*Australian Book Review*

'A powerful and illuminating look at the lot of Australians who have fallen through the cracks in contemporary life … a timely reminder that there is a deep and complicated story of hidden Australia simmering beneath the surface and we are lucky that the brilliant Tony Birch is out there uncovering it for us.'

—*The Saturday Age*

'He is a natural storyteller … In *Common People*, likeable fringe-dwellers slam up against circumstance in sometimes horrific but often moving ways, with inflections of Junot Diaz's *Drown* and John Steinbeck's *Cannery Row*.'

—*Books+Publishing*

'Some of the stories in *Common People* are based on Birch's own personal experiences, but all of them display a striking intimacy with the lingua franca of grit, scrabble, labour. They are stories about mundane and quotidian lives on the margins of Australian society.'

—*Sydney Review of Books*

'Visceral, confronting writing buoyed by humour, easy exchanges of dialogue and unique perspective.'

—*IndigenousX*

'Marvellous … stories of characters whose precarious lives are rebalanced through tiny acts of compassion.'

—*The Sunday Age*

'Short fiction is a singular art, and the stories in *Common People* are tender, raw and extremely well constructed.'

—Maxine Beneba Clarke

'These stories have been distilled to their best parts and finest quality … a collection that stands out for its voice and compassion.'

—Annie Condon, *Readings*

Praise for *The White Girl*

'A profound allegory of good and evil, and a deep exploration of human interaction, black and white, alternately beautiful and tender, cruel and unsettling.'

—*The Guardian*

'The eerie strength of *The White Girl* is the way Birch writes so convincingly on power and the blinding nature of its corruptive forces … He writes social realism, his metier is those who are economically and socially marginalised, and his deep emotional honesty when telling their stories resonates throughout *The White Girl*.'

—*The Sydney Morning Herald*

'A celebration of Aboriginal resilience and kinship in response to trauma. It demands that Australia addresses this savage past.'

—Judges' comments, Miles Franklin Literary Award

Tony Birch is the author of three novels: *The White Girl*, winner of the 2020 NSW Premier's Award for Indigenous Writing, and shortlisted for the 2020 Miles Franklin Literary Award; *Ghost River*, winner of the 2016 Victorian Premier's Literary Award for Indigenous Writing; and *Blood*, which was shortlisted for the Miles Franklin Literary Award in 2012. He is also the author of *Shadowboxing* and four short story collections – *Father's Day*, *The Promise*, *Common People* and *Dark as Last Night* – and has published two poetry collections: *Broken Teeth* and *Whisper Songs*. In 2017 he was awarded the Patrick White Literary Award for his contribution to Australian literature. Tony Birch is also an activist, historian and essayist.

www.tony-birch.com

COMMON
PEOPLE

TONY BIRCH

First published 2017 by University of Queensland Press
PO Box 6042, St Lucia, Queensland 4067 Australia
Reprinted 2017, 2018 (twice), 2019 (twice)

This edition published 2022

University of Queensland Press (UQP) acknowledges the Traditional Owners
and their custodianship of the lands on which UQP operates. We pay our respects
to their Ancestors and their descendants, who continue cultural and spiritual
connections to Country. We recognise their valuable contributions to Australian
and global society.

uqp.com.au
reception@uqp.com.au

Cover design by Jenna Lee
Typeset in Bembo Std by Post Pre-press Group, Brisbane
Printed in Australia by McPherson's Printing Group

Australian Government

University of Queensland Press is assisted by the Australian Government through
the Australia Council, its arts funding and advisory body.

A catalogue record for this book is available from the National Library of Australia.

ISBN 978 0 7022 6582 2 (pbk)
ISBN 978 0 7022 6073 5 (epdf)
ISBN 978 0 7022 6074 2 (epub)
ISBN 978 0 7022 6075 9 (kindle)

University of Queensland Press uses papers that are natural, renewable and
recyclable products made from wood grown in well-managed forests and other
controlled sources. The logging and manufacturing processes conform to the
environmental regulations of the country of origin.

For Isabel Kit

Isabel, Isabel, didn't worry,
Isabel didn't scream or scurry
—Ogden Nash, 'The Adventures of Isabel'

CONTENTS

THE GHOST TRAIN

LYDIA TURNED INTO MARIAN'S DARKENED driveway around eleven, switched off the car's headlights and chewed on her fingernails while she waited. She'd left the house worried she might not get home in time the next morning, doubtful that her fourteen year old would be enthusiastic enough to get himself out of bed for school, let alone his younger sister, who needed to be fed, dressed and dragged to the bus stop.

Lydia popped her head out of the side window when she heard the front door slam and saw her friend's silhouette running towards her. Marian jumped into the passenger seat wearing shorts and a bra. She carried a T-shirt in her hand. She slipped the T-shirt on and Lydia looked across at the face of Barack Obama, his full cheeks aided by Marian's curvaceous breast job, a parting birthday gift from her husband who'd run away with a twenty year old he'd met at the gym six months before. He'd cleaned out the family bank account and re-mortgaged the house to finance a world trip for himself and the new girlfriend. Marian lost the house, and by the time she'd paid off her debts she had nothing to show for fifteen years of marriage except her twin boys and the new boobs.

Lydia reversed out of the driveway, put her foot to the floor and roared out of the street. 'You're late. If we don't get there on time, there'll be no work and this will be a fucking waste of time. Who's taking care of the twins?'

'My sister, Peg. They're at her place. She'll drop them at school in the morning. Anyway, what's the big deal if we're a couple of minutes late? You said yesterday Carlo has it sorted.'

'He does. But only if we're on the line for the shift. Last words he said were *Don't be late*. And you're always fucking late.'

'Okay. Sorry. Give me a cigarette.'

Lydia pointed to Barack Obama. 'Where'd you get that tee? You know that it's about two sizes too small.'

Marian pulled on the front of the T-shirt. 'It's not the top. It's my tits that are too big.' She grabbed a breast in each hand. 'There was a discount on when I got them done. They offered to supersize me for the same price. The old man's eyes lit up when he heard that. He was paying, so I could hardly say no.'

'I'm still asking, who gave it to you, the T-shirt?'

'A fella I've been seeing. He was in the States on business and brought it back.'

'What fella?'

'The IT fella. Justin. You remember Justin?'

'Justin from Adelaide?'

'The one and only.'

'Fucking Justin? The last time he was in town, you never shut up telling me what a lousy fuck he was. He's back?'

'He was here last week. Passing through on the way home to his wife and kids.'

'You're telling me that the same Tinder-man you said was the weakest fuck on the planet went all the way to the United States, came back, called in here for a pit stop with you, and all you got out of the deal was a T-shirt with a picture of the American president on the front? What about some duty-free perfume or jewellery for fuck's sake? You fucked the cheapskate for a *shirt*?'

'I never said I fucked him.'

'You don't have to. I know you fucked him. You have that look on your face.'

'What look?'

'Like you've just fucked a bloke. A shit ride maybe. But a ride.'

Marian ran a fingernail across the word HOPE below the president's face. 'I don't care. I love the T-shirt, and the message. It's saying, you know, don't give up. *Hope.*'

'Are you serious?'

'Yeah. There's nothing wrong with hope, Lydia. Just because you've given up on the world, doesn't mean the rest of us have to. And I like his face. Obama. Have you seen him on the TV? He's fucking beautiful.'

She turned the car radio on and hit the buttons until she found a thumping beat. 'Have you ever slept with a black man?'

Lydia turned onto the highway and headed west. 'I tried to one time when I was pissed. I put the hard word on Carlo. We had a go at it in the back of his car. I was unclipping my bra when he changed his mind. Said he had to think about his wife.'

'What did you say?'

'I told him he could have given her a bit more thought before he got me in his Commodore and stuck his tongue in my mouth and a hand in my pants. He shit himself and begged me not to talk about it.'

'He's probably Catholic. Carlo's from Argentina, isn't he? They're all Catholics over there. Anyway, if you had've fucked him it wouldn't count. He's not black. Carlo is brown.'

'He's as black as that fella on the front of your T-shirt. Anyway, Carlo backing out had nothing to do with him being Catholic. Your ex is a Catholic, isn't he?'

'He is.'

'Well, I reckon he'd fuck a nun.'

'He probably has. Jesus, I hate this song.' Marian pressed the buttons on the radio until she found an old Fleetwood Mac hit. 'And wouldn't she go off?' she laughed.

'Who?'

'The nun. Imagine that. Locked away in a convent for years and getting out for her first ride. She'd light up like a pinball machine.'

'Not if she was stiff enough to end up in bed with my old man. You know they named a movie after him?'

'Which one?'

'*Gone in 60 Seconds*. And that was exaggerating it. More like half a minute. I couldn't pick a decent fuck to save myself.'

They passed the lights of the twenty-four-hour service station and cafe on the highway. 'It should be the next left.' Lydia leaned forward and searched the road through the dirty front windscreen.

'There it is,' Marian shouted. They turned onto a narrow dirt road cutting through unfamiliar country. Marian looked out of the side window. The air was full of dust and insects. 'Where you taking us? Ivan Milat country?'

'Something like that.' Lydia started giggling to herself.

'What are you laughing at?' Marian asked.

'It's nothing.'

'Yes, it is. Come on. Tell me.'

'Ivan Milat.'

'What about him?'

'You heard the joke about him?'

'Nah. And I don't want to hear it.'

'Whatever.'

'Tell me, then.'

'Okay. Ivan Milat picks up this young couple, backpackers hitch-hiking, and drives them into the countryside. He gets them out of his truck and forces them to walk deeper into the bush, where it's dark and creepy. One of the couple he's kidnapped turns to Milat and says, "Hey, it's really scary in here." And Milat, he says, "It sure is. But it's all right for you two. I'm going to have to walk out on my own."'

'That's not funny,' Marian said.

'You don't get the joke?'

'Yeah, I get the joke. And it's not funny. He was a horrible man, and he did terrible things to people.'

'Are you shitting me? Loosen up. You were just telling me I'd given up on life. Jesus, Marian. It's a joke.'

★

They drove on in silence. The countryside was monotonously flat. They passed the occasional light out front of a rundown farmhouse, most likely belonging to an illegal enterprise of one kind or another. The plains were known to police for cockfighting rings, drug labs, dog fights and off-the-grid slaughterhouses. Marian found herself drifting off. She lifted her head in an effort to stay awake. 'What's the pay rate again?'

'Two hundred each, less twenty per cent for the foreman and another five skim for Carlo. The take-home is a hundred and fifty each.'

'Have you packed meat before?'

'Nah. But everything else. Apples. Baby formula. Fertiliser. Shouldn't be a lot different.'

Out of the darkness the dim outline of a row of shipping containers shunted together came into view. Lydia could see the tail lights of cars lined up on the road ahead. She accelerated in an effort to join the convoy. The car skidded from one side of the road to the other. Marian coughed and wound up her window. 'What the fuck are you doing? You'll get us killed before we start.'

'I want to beat the crowd. *Don't be last on the line.* It was the other thing Carlo said to me.'

They parked the car. Other would-be workers were already hurrying towards the open doorway of one of the containers. Slow to get out of the car, Marian ran to catch up with Lydia. The line ahead ground to a halt. Lydia did a quick body count. There were around twenty people in front of them and as many behind, with more people coming.

She turned to Marian and winked. 'We should be okay.'

'Looks like the United Nations are here. You see Carlo?'

'He doesn't have to line up. He's one of the boners. They're royalty in the meat trade.'

Marian poked Lydia in the arse. 'You'd love him boning you.'

Lydia ignored her. She had her eye on a woman, most likely Vietnamese she thought, ahead of them in the line. Lydia wore a singlet and cotton leggings and was soaked with sweat. She stared at the woman's rubber pants. They reminded her of the waders her father used to wear when he went out duck shooting. The line moved forward, through the open door, where each person was handed a number torn from a book of raffle tickets by a man wearing a white dustcoat. The name 'Charlie' was handwritten above a breast pocket.

'Hold onto your tickets,' he barked. One side of the containers was lined with steel benches. On the other, opened cardboard boxes were stacked to ceiling height, ready for use. The line of containers had open doors at each end and went on into the darkness. An argument broke out behind Lydia and Marian. The foreman was trying to close the door on those at the end of the line. 'We've got all we need. Try back tomorrow night.'

A man being pushed out the doorway pleaded with him. 'I drove two hours for this job. I don't even have the petrol money to get home. *Please.*'

Charlie leaned forward and spoke quietly in the man's ear. He nodded his head and Charlie allowed him to join the end of the line before bolting the door and inspecting the crowd. He stopped in front of Marian and looked down at her bare legs. His tongue rested on his bottom lip. He looked up, stared at her breasts and pointed to Barack Obama's bulbous cheeks.

'Are you political or something?'

Marian nervously patted one breast. 'No. Not me.'

'Good. You girls together?' he asked Lydia.

'Yeah.'

He licked his bottom lip. 'A couple?'

Lydia couldn't help herself. 'You wish,' she answered.

'What's that?' he snapped. 'We don't put up with any smart-arses here. Are you a smart-arse, girl?'

Lydia wanted to tell him to go fuck his fat self. She said nothing and looked down at the floor.

He stopped again, in front of the next worker in line, the Vietnamese woman. 'Good to see you, Mary. You my worker number one,' he mocked.

'I'm not Mary. It's Rose,' she answered.

'Mary. Rose. Same difference,' he shrugged.

He completed the muster, walked across the room and knocked at the glass door of a small office. 'They're ready,' Charlie said to a man whose own dustcoat identified him as the manager. He inspected the line, grouping workers together. 'These two on the freezer. Next four, packing at the boning table. Two on the steam hose ...'

The manager reached Lydia and Marian. 'I haven't seen you before. You have a name for me?'

'Carlo,' Lydia answered.

'Did he go over the rate with you?'

'Yep.'

8

'And the carve up?'

'Yep.'

'Good,' he smiled, and turned to Charlie. 'Put them on packing with this one,' he ordered, pointing to the Vietnamese woman. 'You two,' he said to Lydia, 'follow what she does. And try keeping up with her.'

He took Charlie aside and spoke quietly to him. 'The last on the line, you explain the terms to him?'

'He's happy enough being picked up. The man's desperate.'

'Good. Put him out back on the barrel.'

'We have a truck coming in?'

'From New South Wales. They shit themselves when the live baiting story got out. Talk about a slaughter. It's carnage up there. They've been spending more on bullets than feed.'

The workers were shuffled into a second room, where their raffle tickets were handed to a woman at a desk. She made a note of each ticket number, photocopied IDs of any new faces, and pointed to a pile of white overalls and rubber boots in the corner. The overalls Marian picked up were several sizes too big. She couldn't help but laugh at how ridiculous she and Lydia looked.

'Hey, *I'm bringing sexy back*,' she sang.

She hadn't noticed that Charlie, the foreman, was standing in the doorway watching the women change.

'Come on, girls. Let's not fuck around. The boners are at the tables ready to go. There's a toilet if you need it. Take a break only if you have to, and keep up if you want to come back another night.'

★

The boners, each wearing an apron and a knife belt, stood at the row of steel tables, while other workers, shouldering sides of beef, marched the aisles dumping a carcass in front of each boner. Lydia and Marian watched in astonishment as the men, including Carlo, who winked across the room at Lydia, went to work with precision, slicing each carcass into a range of cuts: shoulders, legs, hind quarters and steaks. The meat was transferred to the tables, where it was packed, sealed and labelled. Rose instructed Lydia and Marian what to do, mostly through her actions. She collected an empty box, stood it on one end and began packing beef shoulders into it.

'You and you. Do the same.'

The women followed her lead, but struggled to keep pace. When she'd finished packing, Rose sealed the box with tape, placed a sticker on each side of the box, indicating the cut of meat inside, and loaded it onto a trolley. As each trolley was filled another worker pushed it out of the room to the portable freezer where it was shelved, ready for transport. Marian found packing the meat relatively easy but couldn't lift the full box across to the trolley and needed Lydia's help. Charlie, watching closely, walked over to the women.

'You'll need to speed it up. Mary here is leaving you two for dead.'

Marian waited until he was far enough away before whispering to Lydia, 'Cunt.' She glanced over at Rose. 'The woman is a machine. I can't keep up with her.'

'Maz,' Lydia panted, 'please shut it. Keep your head down and do the best you can.'

But Marian wouldn't shut up. 'Look at those pants she's wearing. You know what they'd be for?'

Lydia strained under the weight of a box of steaks and dumped it on the trolley. 'I said shut it. I don't give a fuck about her pants.'

'I bet she pisses in them so she doesn't have to take a toilet break.'

'She'll hear you,' Lydia hissed.

'Hear all she likes. Probably can't understand a word I'm saying.'

After two hours of packing Marian had worn herself out and worked in silence. Lydia's arms burned each time she lifted a box onto the trolley. Desperate to go to the toilet she looked around the room. Neither the foreman nor the manager were anywhere to be seen.

'Marian, I need to have a piss.'

'Really?' She blew a fringe of hair out of her eyes. 'You should ask your friend here if you can borrow her pants.'

'Where'd that fella Charlie say the toilet was?'

'He didn't. It would be where we got changed, I'd reckon.'

Lydia left the bench and ran across to the door to the changeroom. She couldn't see a toilet and walked through a pair of saloon doors and out onto an open platform. She was hit by a terrible smell. The worker who'd been picked up last on the line was dragging a carcass from a truck. His overalls were covered in blood and mud and shit. The animal had been skinned and the ears had been cut off. The back of the truck was loaded with more carcasses.

'What are you doing?' Lydia asked, covering her mouth with the back of her hand.

'Same as you. Working.'

Lydia looked down at the animal. She felt sick. 'What is it?'

'This one? Probably the dog I did twenty dollars on a couple of months back.'

'Why have his ears been cut off?'

'Greyhounds get tattoos inside both ears soon after they're born.'

'Why?'

'For identity purposes. Hacking them off, a dog can't be traced back to the owner.'

'A greyhound? That's not meat.'

'Soon will be. Watch this.'

The worker picked up the carcass, straining under its weight, and dropped it into the barrel of a machine. He hit a button on the side of the machine and stood back. The crunching of bones and flesh soon reduced the carcass to mince. Unable to stop herself, Lydia fell to her knees and vomited over the edge of the platform. Resting on all fours she breathed in and out.

'What are you doing out here?'

She looked up at the manager. He had one eye on her and the other on the truckload of slaughtered dogs. The putrid air was making her feel worse.

'Nothing. I was taking my toilet break.' She got to her feet and wiped her hand across her mouth.

'What's wrong? You can't take the smell of raw meat?'

'It's not that. I've had a cold is all. I'll be fine.'

'You shouldn't be out here. There's a women's toilet inside.'

'Sorry, I didn't see it. I must have headed the wrong way.'

The barrel started up again. Both Lydia and the manager

ignored the sound of breaking bones. He escorted her back inside. 'You enjoying the work?'

'Yeah. It's fine.'

The manager rested a hand on her waist. 'There's guaranteed work here if you want it.'

Lydia brushed his hand away, walked off and found the toilet.

'You okay?' Marian asked, when Lydia returned to the packing table. 'You've turned fucking grey.'

'I'm fine. Just needed some fresh air.'

'Something happen back there?'

'Yeah. I had a piss and washed my hands. Leave me be.'

The sun was about to rise by the time Lydia and Marian headed for the car, one hundred and fifty dollars cash each in their pockets. They were exhausted. Lydia's shoulders were aching and Marian's face was smeared with animal blood. As was Barack Obama's. Lydia saw Rose standing at the back of her car, a battered station wagon. She opened the rear door and climbed inside. Lydia and Marian stood watching as Rose reached deep into her rubber wading pants. She pulled out a variety of prime cuts of meat, sealed and labelled. They quickly filled a large esky. Rose hopped out of the wagon, unbuckled the wading pants and threw them into the back of the car. She looked at Marian and smiled a little nervously. Reaching back into the esky Rose brought out two parcels of meat. She looked at Lydia's worn-out face. 'This is for you,' she offered.

Lydia looked around the car park and stuck the parcel of meat under her T-shirt. 'Thank you. Rose?'

'Yep, it's Rose,' she answered in a clear accent. 'My father chose the name from the lid of a chocolate box when we came here.'

Rose turned to Marian and offered her the second parcel of meat.

Although she felt a little guilty for doing so, Marian took the meat. 'Thanks.'

Rose looked at Barack Obama's bloodied cheeks and smiled. 'Your boyfriend there. He's a mess.'

HARMLESS

I WANT TO TELL YOU A STORY ABOUT HARMLESS, which wasn't his *true* name, although it was the only one I knew him by. *There goes Harmless*, people would say when he walked by in the street. And Harmless was just that. *Harmless*. He was a little strange too, but always minded his own business, circling the town on foot, talking to nobody but himself. People would sometimes offer him help, but Harmless didn't want help, and let them know without speaking a word. He used to sleep nights in the bandstand in the middle of the park, except on cold and wet winter nights, when the police would drive by and insist he take up their offer of a bed, a blanket and a hot meal.

One night some hard boys from the city, passing through town and out for trouble, spotted Harmless in the park walking back to his cubby. They followed him and gave him a furious belting. Afterwards, two of the boys pissed in his face while Harmless lay on the ground. They were long gone out of town before he was discovered the next morning staggering down the street with a bloodied head and black eye. Although nobody from our town had been responsible, Harmless decided he'd had enough of us and took off. For weeks nobody knew where he'd gone. Some thought he was dead. A story went around that he'd filled his pockets with rocks, thrown himself into the river and drowned.

But Harmless wasn't dead. After leaving the hospital the day after he was beaten up, he'd quietly walked out of town along the railway line until he reached the trestle bridge. He crossed it and followed an old track through the bush to a timber cutter's shack that hadn't been used in years. It was a month later before Harmless turned up again, scrawny and desperate for a feed. Mr Mercer, the boss of the only supermarket in town, saw Harmless walking by, stopped him on the street and handed him a canteen of water, a loaf of bread and a bag of fresh fruit. He went back inside the supermarket and called the police.

The sergeant, Mick Potter, who was also coach of the football team, found Harmless sitting on a bench outside the town hall and invited him to the station for a hot shower and cup of tea. Harmless took up the offer but wouldn't tell Mick where he'd been and refused the sergeant's offer of staying at the police station until a proper bed could be found for him. Harmless agreed to come into town once a week and collect a bag of groceries, toilet paper and soap from the police station. In return, he asked Mick to add a weekly newspaper to the deal. The two men shook on the agreement and even though he wore no watch, from that day on Harmless would turn up at the police station at twelve noon every Wednesday. Each time he'd double and triple back through the bush to his shack, giving the slip to anyone who might try to track him, although no one ever bothered until the day I followed him home.

On my thirteenth birthday my grandmother took me down to the garage and bought me a second-hand bicycle. There were two on sale that morning. One was a three-speed racer that had been oiled, fitted with new tyres and a frame sprayed black by Harry Huntly, the owner of the garage. The other bike was a girl's model, hot pink, with a new cushioned seat and streamers on the handlebars. Once I'd ridden both bikes around the garage I went for the black one. My nanna wasn't happy with my choice.

'The black one? Look at this pink bike. It's beautiful. Harry's done a real job with them streamers.'

Harry was as surprised as Nan. The pink bike was twenty dollars more expensive. He was thinking I'd picked the black bike to save my grandmother money.

'Look. I'll knock the twenty off. You can have it for the same price as the black one. Thirteen, that's a teenager's birthday,' he winked. 'A special one.'

I wouldn't have taken the pink bike if Harry had offered it to me for free. I wore my hair short in those days, never wore pink and wasn't interested in a bicycle that looked *pretty*.

'It's not the money, Nan,' I said. 'I like the other bike.'

She raised her eyebrows. 'Please yourself then. It looks like a copper's bike to my eyes. But it's your birthday.'

I was hardly off my black bike from that day on. I became a free bird, criss-crossing the miles of gravel road alongside the irrigation channels surrounding town, always on my own. As it was, most girls from school avoided me anyway. Although I didn't mind playing alone, one day I'd asked the girl who sat next to me in Year Six, Lara Conner, why the other girls ignored me.

'Well, you're just too much of a tomboy,' she explained, apologetically.

I was confused. 'Like how?'

'Well, like playing in the yard rougher than the boys. And wearing boys' shorts. And having your hair cut the way you do. If you grow your hair long, maybe you'll fit in more.'

I thought Lara was stupid, but was polite enough not to say so. I wasn't going to grow my hair long just to find a friend. And I liked wearing shorts, which I knew, even back then, would stop the boys from looking up your dress at your *Annie*, as my nan preferred to call *it*.

'I don't play any rougher than the boys do.'

'That's not the point. You shouldn't be playing rough at all.'

It was true that I could run faster and further than most boys in school. I could also punch as hard as any of them. Most boys were afraid of me so I never got teased. And they didn't pull my hair or pinch my arm in the line at morning assembly.

Riding my bike one Wednesday during the winter school holidays, I saw Harmless walking along the railway line carrying his grocery bag. I rode downhill and stopped by the river and watched as he crossed the trestle bridge. Looking up, I could see him through the gaps in the wooden sleepers. Once he was on the other side, I hopped off my bike and walked it across the bridge to be sure I'd make no noise. Harmless was up ahead of me. He took to a dirt track, too narrow to fit myself and the bike. I wheeled the bike into the bush and lay it in the long grass, satisfied it was well hidden. A little further on, the track ended at a small wooden shack. Harmless opened the door and went inside. I wanted to knock and say hello, tell him I was sorry for what the city boys had done to him. But I didn't. I understood enough about Harmless to accept he didn't like company and might get angry with me for following him.

I went home that night and thought about Harmless and how he got by alone. I was desperate to get inside his hut and see how he lived. A week later I again waited under the bridge for him to pass by. Once he'd crossed the bridge and headed into town I hid my bike in the same place I'd left it the week before and ran all the way to his shack. The door was bolted but not locked. I opened it and went inside. There was a mattress on the floor with two blankets folded neat as handkerchiefs on top. The room was bare except for a wooden chair, a kettle, a tin mug, a plate, two bent forks and different sized spoons. A pot-belly stove sat in one corner. I touched the steel chimney with the back of my hand. It was warm.

The shack Harmless lived in might not have been what most people would want, but it was clean and tidy, out of the way of snoops, and as homely as any place I'd been in. He'd decorated inside, sticking photographs from old newspapers on the walls, mostly of famous people. The Queen of England's picture was plastered up beside the door. She was sitting between a photograph of The Beatles and another of a racehorse biting into a birthday cake. I sat on the mattress and rested my head on his pillow. The wind rattled sheets of iron, followed by rain beating on the roof. I lay down and covered myself with one of the blankets. I'd often felt sad for Harmless, thinking that his life was lonely and miserable, but laying in his bed and listening to the rain I understood that he had made his own life, one he owned.

When I woke I had no idea where I was. I sat upright, full of fear, until I looked above me and saw the Queen, tiara on her head, smiling down at me. I quickly folded the blanket and ran through the rain to my bike. I rode all the way home without once touching the seat. Nan looked at me suspiciously when I got in. I was soaked through and my cheeks were flushed red.

'Where have you been, young missy?' she asked. 'Other than out chasing a bout of pneumonia?'

'Down the river,' I shrugged, as if I'd been up to nothing of importance.

'Oh, yeah. Down the river doing what?'

'Looking for frogs and tadpoles. It's science homework.'

She looked at me over the top of her glasses and smiled. 'You don't do much homework during the term, let alone the holidays. You sure?'

'Sure, Nan,' I answered, without blinking.

She gave me a long stare before accepting she wasn't going to get anything more out of me. 'You wash your face and hands and set the table. Then we'll give thanks for the meal and pretend you're a good girl for a bit.'

The winters in our town are the wettest in the state. We're east of the mountains and when clouds build over the range and grow dark and heavy, they dump buckets of rain on us. The streets sometimes flood, as do the irrigation channels and creeks. Country can disappear for weeks at a time. Following one storm, Nan took me further into the bush than we'd been before and showed me a waterfall running red. She told me the land was bleeding because people treated it badly. Although I wouldn't talk to anyone about it, in case they said my nan was crazy and I'd have to fight them, I knew every word she spoke was the truth.

It never mattered to me how heavy the rain got, it was never bad enough to stop me riding my bike. I would often arrive home after pedalling around in the wet all day with the bike caked in mud and a streak of red running up the back of my jumper. Nan was one for rules and wouldn't let me in the house until I'd hosed the bike down on the back grass and cleaned it. Once the bike was in order I would wheel it onto the verandah where it was safe. The house was out of bounds until I stripped down to my underwear.

About a week after I'd snuck into Harmless's shack, the rain thumped on our roof all night and didn't stop until morning. I knew the river would be thundering and had to see it. After breakfast, I jumped on my bike and followed the river downstream until I reached the trestle bridge. I hit the brakes when I spotted Laurie Wise's orange panel van parked underneath. Everyone knew Laurie. He came from a wild family and was always in trouble with the police. He'd sometimes drive through the main street on a Saturday night, calling out to the girls, whistling to them, trying to get them into the van. I heard my nan talking over the fence one time to our neighbour, Dotty Pearce. Laurie had been in a fight in the middle of town, and Dotty and Nan had words over him.

'The boy is just plain stupid,' Dotty said.

'I wish that was all he was,' Nan answered. 'He's dangerous. Laurie is going to seriously hurt someone one of these days. Being stupid is no excuse for being cruel and a bully. And that's what he is.'

Dotty continued her defence of Laurie. 'How could you expect any more of him? They say his father has a metal plate in his head.'

'I don't care what sort of plate the father has in that head of his. It could be made of cardboard for all I care. Laurie behaving the way he does is his own responsibility, not that of his idiotic family.'

I went to turn my bike around and was about to pedal uphill when I heard the van door creak open. I stopped and looked back. Laurie was getting out. He walked to the other side of the car, opened the door and swore at someone sitting in the passenger seat. He reached into the van and dragged out a girl. She fell to her knees. I could see by her long red hair the girl was Rita Collins. She lived on a farm outside town and was in the year above me but had been taken out of school by her mother only weeks after the new term started and hadn't been seen in town since. Rita was only fourteen.

I pushed my bike behind some blackberry on the side of the track, hid and watched. Laurie screamed at Rita to stand up. When she did I could see she had an enormous belly.

But not like she was fat. Rita was pregnant. Thunder crashed above me and the rain came down again, as heavy as it had been in the night. Laurie pointed a finger at Rita and pushed her. She pushed back. And then he hit her. Not like a kid might do to another kid on a street corner. Laurie was almost a man, and she was only a girl, and he punched her so hard in the face she fell to the ground. He stood over her, swore again and told her to get up. She kept her head down and didn't move. He put a boot against her shoulder, let it rest and said something I couldn't hear on account of the rain. He pushed her with the heel of the boot. She fell onto her side and lay in the dirt. Laurie turned his back on her, got into the van and roared away.

I ducked behind the blackberry bushes and listened. Rita was moaning. I stuck my head up. She'd lifted her dress around her waist and seemed to be searching between her legs for something. She didn't see me at all until I was standing next to her. Rita covered her face with a hand and was quick to duck her head, as if I was somebody who had come to hurt her, too. I called her name, quiet, so as not to frighten her. She might not have known who I was, but at least I wasn't Laurie Wise.

'I'm going to have a baby,' she cried.

'I know that,' I said. 'I seen pregnant bellies before. When will you be having your one?'

She moaned again and reached between her legs with her hand. 'I think now.'

We both stared at her hand. It was covered in blood. She lifted it up to her face and the blood, pelted by rain, ran down her arm. It looked bad enough to frighten me.

'You have to go to the hospital,' I said. 'If you want, I can ride my bike home and tell my nan to bring a doctor here.'

She moaned again and began to cry. 'Oh, fuck. It's going to come. *Now.*'

If a baby was going to come Rita had to get out of the rain and mud. I looked up at the trestle bridge. The only place close by was Harmless's hut. 'You'd better come with me.'

'Where to?'

I held out my hand. 'Away from here. Laurie could come back.'

Rita put her hand in mine. I helped her to stand. She leaned on me as we walked up to the bridge, getting belted by the weather, slipping in the mud. While it was slow going, at least her pain seemed to have stopped.

She looked at me closely as we crossed the bridge. 'I know you. From school.'

'You too,' I smiled. 'I know you.'

'Where are you taking me?'

'Just along here. Out of the rain.'

'But there's nothing up here.'

We were on the narrow dirt track when she moaned again. She put both hands between her legs. Liquid ran down her thighs. It was the colour of milk.

'Stop. I need to lay down,' she said.

I could see smoke rising from the chimney of the shack. 'We can't stop. Not yet,' I told her and yanked her by the arm. 'Just a little further.'

I knocked at the door. Not too loud. When Harmless didn't answer I knocked harder and called out to him. 'Mr Harmless, we need your help.'

Rita put one arm below her stomach, rested her head in the other hand and leaned against the door with all her weight. It swung open so quickly she fell into the room. Harmless jumped up from his mattress. From a distance I'd always thought he must be an old man. Up close he looked much younger, almost a boy. His skin was unmarked and his brown eyes were as soft as my nan's. He looked down at Rita and up at me, like I needed to provide him with an explanation.

'She's having a baby,' was all I could say. 'And I think it's coming.'

He frowned. I thought that maybe he hadn't understood what I'd said. But then he reached down, grabbed Rita by the arms and dragged her into the room, onto the mattress. The pot-belly stove pushed out its warmth. Harmless threw a blanket over Rita's shivering body and stood back. He didn't know what to do for her any more than I did. She screamed and swore and slapped her own thighs and kicked and even spat. I was so afraid I huddled in a corner, closed my eyes and covered my ears. A little while later I heard a cry and knew it couldn't be Rita. I looked up and saw Harmless, kneeling at Rita's feet, holding something in his arms. It wriggled and squirmed and was pink and bloody. It was a newborn baby.

Rita lay on her back. She was worn out by all the effort and couldn't move. Harmless looked down at the baby.

'Should I go and get someone?' I asked him.

Harmless said nothing, as if he was under a spell.

I ran from the shack and back across the bridge to where I'd dumped my bike. I pedalled fast enough to burn the muscles in my legs, riding all the way to the hospital on the other side of town. I couldn't speak when I got there, until a nurse was able to calm me down. I explained about Rita and Harmless and the baby.

It took a lot of effort for the ambulance men to cross the bridge on foot, carrying a stretcher, blankets and medicines. Harmless was sitting on the floor with the baby in his arms. A bloodied rope was attached to the baby's stomach. Rita hadn't moved from the mattress. One ambulance man examined her and the other one spoke quietly to Harmless. 'I need you to carry the baby, in the blanket you have her wrapped in. We'll take Mum on the stretcher and you will follow. Is that okay?'

Harmless closely watched the ambulance man and nodded his head as the rope was cut from the baby's body.

At the hospital, Rita and the baby were taken away. A nurse asked me and Harmless to sit and wait on a bench while she telephoned the police. 'I'm sure they will need to speak to you,' she said. Harmless looked straight ahead and ignored her. I wanted to thank him for what he'd done but was too shy.

He tapped me on the knee. 'You ride the black bicycle,' he said, speaking slowly, almost stopping on each word. 'I seen you following me.'

'Sorry, I wanted to see where you lived,' I answered. 'I'm really sorry. My nan is always telling me not to be a snoop.'

The nurse came back to tell us that the police were only five minutes away.

'Is there anything I can get you two?' she asked. 'A sandwich and a cup of tea?'

I couldn't think of anything I needed. Harmless said nothing but watched her mouth closely as she spoke. When the nurse left, Harmless stood up. He smiled down at me and walked straight through the automatic doors and out of the hospital. If I didn't have a nan at home who loved me, I'd have followed him.

The next day the police sergeant, Mick Potter, found his way to the cutter's shack and knocked at the door. Harmless wasn't around. The local paper decided to write a story on what had happened and the reporter wanted to interview Harmless and take his photograph. The reporter couldn't find him either. The newspaper asked to interview me as well. I was excited by the idea of having my name and picture in the paper but Nan wouldn't hear of it. She told me that no good could come from making a *public spectacle* of myself. She sat me down in the kitchen and told me about Harmless. He was deaf, had always been so, but could lip-read perfectly.

'He's got a gift,' she said.

'What's that?'

'Well, when he doesn't want to listen to people all he has to do is turn away or close his eyes.'

Weeks later I saw Rita Collins walking along the street pushing her baby in a pram. I called out to her but she walked by as if I didn't exist. It wasn't long after that she was seen riding around in Laurie Wise's van. She never said a word to the sergeant about Laurie punching her in the face. And she told nobody who the father of her baby was. I kept my mouth shut and said nothing either. It made no difference. The town knew, as it always did. Eventually Rita and Laurie got together. They got special permission to marry when she was sixteen. Laurie moved out to the farmhouse and worked for Rita's father. She had another two babies, little more than a year apart. I saw her in town now and then, often wearing a faded black eye behind a decent caking of make-up.

The year of Rita's twenty-first birthday Laurie was electrocuted by a fallen wire while driving a harvester along the highway. The electric company was at fault and paid Rita enough money for her to buy her own house in town and put herself through college. Whenever Nan saw her down the street after that she'd smile at me and say, 'How lucky is that girl?'

Harmless was never seen in town again. To this day nobody knows where he got to. Months after he vanished I rode out to the shack and knocked politely at his door, which he wouldn't have heard anyway on account of his deafness. I knew in my heart he'd not be home. I went inside and looked up at the faded picture of the Queen of England. I turned the mattress over to hide Rita's stain that had since turned brown. I picked up an old broom, swept the shack floor and loaded the pot-belly stove with kindling and paper. I lit the fire, sat down and waited for the room to warm.

DEATH STAR

MANY YEARS EARLIER THE TOWN FATHERS voted to commemorate the war dead of the district with an Avenue of Honour. A mournful sentry of ghost gums was planted stretching along both sides of the highway just south of the town. Each tree represented the life of a young soldier *fallen in battle*. The trees grew tall and healthy. No one at the time could have predicted they'd become the site for more young deaths, drawing speeding cars and the bodies of teenagers like moths to a deadly flame. Roadside memorials – hand-painted white crosses, photographs, stuffed toys and unopened bottles of whiskey and beer – accumulated over the years to mark the carnage.

At a bend on the highway, opposite the front gate of Telford's dairy, sat the darkened trunk of one of the greatest of the memorial trees. Dominic Cross would often take the hour-long walk from home and place his open hand against the deep scar in the tree trunk, which still bled thick sap from a gaping wound more than a year after the accident that killed his older brother.

Patrick Cross left the highway sometime around dawn, behind the wheel of a reconditioned Torana XU1. The model was an original legendary 'suicide machine', equipped with an engine too powerful for the young car thieves who coveted them. Old Mr Telford, heading back to his farmhouse after morning milking, heard a car gunning along the highway off in the distance. As the engine drew closer the vibration of its deep roar rattled the line of wire ribboning the farm fence. The car hit the bend, left the black-iced bitumen and ascended into the morning mist in a moment of grace that defied the imminent tragedy. The car slammed into the tree, wrapped itself around the trunk and exploded into flames. Telford watched in horror as the car burned, blackening the tree trunk. He returned to the farmhouse and telephoned the police, and later that morning stood on his front verandah nursing a mug of tea, watching as the burnt and mangled body of the driver was cut from the wreck.

Dominic hid from the world on the day of his brother's funeral. The night before, his mother had laid out a black suit, white shirt and polished shoes for him to wear. When he failed to answer the knock at his bedroom door the next morning, she opened it. Dominic had vanished, and the suit that she'd laid out for him on the empty bed opposite was still where she'd left it. She searched the house for her son but couldn't locate him. The boy's father went looking for him in the unruly back garden and lean-to garage along the side of the house without finding him. When Dominic was younger he'd often hidden in the garage, playing alone, inventing a world for himself from scraps of wood and lengths of irrigation pipe. Unknown to his parents, Dominic had climbed the back fence in the early hours of the morning and run along the dirt track following the creek bed out of town. He didn't stop until he reached the fruit cannery where he and Pat had once spent their weekends, a pair of tricksters on BMX bikes, racing the length of the loading dock and leaping into thin air.

In the end his parents had no choice but to leave in the funeral car without him.

The news of Dominic's disappearance did not go unnoticed at the wake, which was held at the local football club changing rooms. Jed Carter, one of the pallbearers, had ridden with Pat. He was a hot-wire specialist and could break into a car and turn the engine over within seconds. As the wake wound down Jed volunteered to a weary Mrs Cross to help find Dominic. He knew where to look. Jed had punished his own bike at the cannery yard when he was a kid and had helped the Cross brothers build a ramp off one end of the loading bay.

Jed left the football club, beer in hand, and walked out to the old factory. He found Dominic sitting on the loading dock dangling his feet over the edge. Hearing him approach, Dominic lay back on the rough concrete and looked up at the sky. Jed tried climbing onto the dock and fell backwards onto his arse. He was drunk.

'Whoa,' he laughed. 'I've had it. Too many beers. What are you doing here, Dom? Your mum's worrying herself sick over you. And your old man. Every beer he downs he's talking more about the belting you're going to get from him when you get in. Why didn't you front for the service? We're talking about your own brother here.'

Dominic rested his hands behind his head. 'Because I didn't want to.'

Jed hauled himself onto the dock, brushing the dirt from the knees of his cheap suit, and sat alongside Dominic. 'Fair enough. My older brother, Frank, when he went, I never wanted to go to the funeral either. They made me, my folks. Wish I hadn't.'

Dominic flipped over onto his stomach. 'Why was that?'

'We'll, he'd been in the water for three days before they found him by dragging a long net downriver. Scooped him out like some rotten old king carp. Jesus, he was fucked. His face, and the rest of him. The yabbies had fed off him. They should have screwed the lid of the coffin down tight.'

Jed looked into the neck of his bottle of beer, took a drink and stared across the empty paddocks, to the sentry of trees on the highway swaying in the breeze.

'My mother, I still can't believe this, she had words with the priest and they decided to keep the coffin open. Trigg, from the funeral parlour, he did what he could to get Frank looking decent. He puttied the holes where he'd been eaten around the face. Even put lipstick on him. I remember that. Mum grabbed me by the arm and marched me to the altar, where the coffin was. Fuck me. I could hardly recognise him. I reckon she was trying to scare me, to stop me fucking around.'

'Was my brother's coffin open?' Dominic asked.

'Nah. Thank God. They say he was too …'

'Burned up?'

'Yeah. And more.'

Dominic didn't appear upset about his brother's death, but it was hard to know, Jed thought. Generations of Cross boys were known for their toughness.

Dominic sat up. 'He was driving no bomb. And it wasn't a local car. Where'd he get hold of an XU1?'

'Out at the country club. It belonged to some tourist up for the golf and the pokies. Fucken golf. What a joke.' Jed finished off his beer and hurled the bottle into the paddock.

'I would've been in the car with him Sunday morning except my old man ordered me to drive out west with him in the truck on Saturday night. We were supposed to be onto a bull run, but we couldn't find the bastard. We came home with one dud milking cow and a pair of goats. He slaughtered the goats in the yard Sunday arvo and fed the meat to the dogs.'

'What did he do with the cow, if it's not milking?'

'He's taken a shine to it. Says we'll keep it.'

'You and Pat been racing or selling?'

'Both. It depended if an order came in. A high-end motor's worth a lot more in cash than drag racing some yahoo fuckwit out at the fire road.'

'Who were you selling to?'

Jed was desperate for another drink. 'Walk down to the bottleshop with me and I'll tell you about it.'

Jed bought a bottle of whiskey, staggered across to the playground opposite the bottleshop and squeezed himself into a kiddies swing. He unscrewed the bottle and threw the cap at a rusted sign: *Tidy Town – 1978.*

'You know George Barron who runs the scrap yard?'

'Sure. He ran stock cars at the drag track for years. Dad used to take us out there on Saturday nights.'

Jed took a long swig from the whiskey bottle, a desperate man dying of thirst.

'About six months back we were out at the yard, Pat and me, chasing a steering wheel for my Commodore. I could hardly believe it when we found one. We pulled it out with the tools, walked over to George's hut by the gate and I asked, "How much for this?" He said nothing for a minute. I thought the cunt had gone deaf and asked him again. He winked at me and said, "Be patient, son, I'm thinking." Another couple of minutes went by and he said we could have the steering wheel for free, plus any other spare parts we wanted off the wreck. It was a good deal, but there was a catch.'

'What was it?'

'He said he wanted us to lift an Audi for him. "Like fuck," I told him. There's nobody in this town who drives an Audi. "It's a city car," I said.'

Jed took another drink from the bottle and swung back and forth on the swing.

'Shifty old George was about twenty steps ahead of us. He told us some fella had been coming up to the country club from Melbourne most weekends for a wrestle in the cot with some woman he was having it off with. "He drives a beautiful midnight blue Audi," George said. "You get me that car and we're in business, boys." The information on the car checked out. Around three the next Sunday morning me and Pat were watching the car from the rise above the car park. It was dead quiet except for a couple of drunks rolling out of the pokies. We waited until they were gone. All we had to do was stroll down to the car park and take it. We were out of there in three minutes, and back at George's in ten.'

'Why would George Barron want you to steal a flash car like an Audi, and strip it down for spare parts?'

'That's not how it works. George moves the cars to the city in shipping containers, working with a syndicate down there. The night we drove in with the Audi, Pat told him to stick the spare parts deal he'd offered. He asked for a thousand each. George didn't blink. He paid us in cash that night. We've been dealing with him ever since. And three weeks ago we hit the jackpot. A two-door Mercedes. Close to new. You should have seen George's face when we drove it into the yard. Looked like he was about to drop his pants and pull himself.'

'How much did you get for it?'

'Nothing. Not yet. We asked for two-five each and he started complaining about *cash flow* or something. Whoever he works with in the city owes George. Or so he says. He's waiting on them, and we were waiting on him. Five thousand dollars. Pat's half is yours, Dom.'

Dominic spat on the ground. 'I don't think I want the money. If Pat hadn't been knocking cars for George, he'd be alive.'

'Maybe. And maybe not. You know the way your brother was. He'd lift a car for money. And he'd steal one just so he could wind the windows down and roar along the highway at night. I don't want to be disrespectful, but he had a death wish, Dom.'

'Bullshit. The road was iced that morning. Could have happened to anyone.'

'You can believe me or not. He was your brother and you need to believe whatever sits comfortable with you. I get that.' He held up the half-empty whiskey bottle. 'Fuck. I threw the top away.'

Jed got up from the swing and searched the ground until he found the screw-on cap.

'I'm gonna drive over to George's yard tomorrow and tell him I'm not waiting any longer for the money. If you don't want Pat's share give it to your folks to help pay for the funeral.'

'I better be going. Might as well get my arse kicked by the old man tonight instead of sleeping on it. Hey, why are you telling me about the money you're owed from Barron? You could keep the lot for yourself. No one would know.'

'I might be a car thief, Dom. But I'm not fucken dishonest.'

Dominic left the playground with his brother on his mind. Until Pat became addicted to stealing cars, the Cross boys had been inseparable. They shared a bedroom at home, were only a year apart at school, and played on the same football team. Nights were taken up with a fire in the backyard, sharing stories, often ghost tales Pat had invented to frighten his little brother. But when Pat discovered fast cars and a partner in Jed, who was just as eager, he left the backyard and his brother behind. When Dominic reached the far corner of the park he turned around. Jed was laying across a swing and twirling his body around in circles the way a kid would do.

*

Barron's scrap yard sat at the end of a stretch of gravel road. Jed had borrowed his father's truck, with the explanation that he'd picked up a landscaping job and Dominic was going to be working with him for the day. He skidded and fishtailed along the road, kicking up gravel and dust. George Barron had inherited the scrap business from his father along with a reasonable bank balance after the old man was crushed under the stock car engine he was working on. George rewarded his good fortune by drinking day and night. It took him a little over a year to run the business into the ground. Soon after, word spread through the stolen car trade that George Barron was ready to move illegal stock. Whether he'd approached the *cut and shut* syndicate in the city or they'd called him, he was soon open for business to anyone able to get their hands on late model cars, with imports fetching a premium price.

The boys walked through an iron gate into the scrap yard and knocked at the open door of the shed that passed for an office. There was no answer. 'Come on,' Jed said. 'Let's go in.' The walls inside were plastered with posters of naked women. Spare engine parts were piled on a narrow desk in one corner and stacked on shelves behind the desk, a complete V8 motor sat in the centre of the room. Dominic heard a toilet flush. George appeared at a curtained doorway hitching up his pants.

'What do you want here?' George barked, not bothering to buckle his belt. 'Nobody comes in here without my say-so.'

'I'm here for the money you owe me,' Jed said. 'Mine and Pat's. You need to pay us for the Mercedes.'

'Fucking Pat,' George laughed. 'Let's not worry too much about having to pay Pat. He fucked himself good and proper.

There's no coin heading his way. What would he spend it on? Angel wings?' he chuckled.

Dominic's feet shifted in the gravel.

'Knock it off,' Jed said. 'This is Dom, Pat's brother.'

'Oh, pardon me. I'm very sorry,' George said, with little sincerity. 'I'm sorry about the business that went on with your brother. He was a good worker. I'm sorry to be losing him.'

'He never worked for you and neither did I,' Jed snapped. 'We were in a business arrangement. And you owe us.'

George threw his hands in the air. 'I don't have the money for you, son. Not yet. I've had no luck moving the Merc. I got it sitting under a tarp in the workshop. I told you before, I can't pay you until I'm paid. It's been a short couple of weeks for all of us. I've got a couple of beauties back there, ready to go, but business is quiet in the city. The larceny squad are sniffing around like fucken gun dogs. My pockets are empty until I move these two cars on. Be patient and give it another week. We'll come good. Both of us.'

'We dropped the car here three weeks ago. Pat reckoned you probably sold it already and you're holding out.'

'Sold it? If you don't fucken believe me come out back. I can show you the car.'

'Why can't you pay now?' Jed asked. 'We've delivered on time. You can easy get your money when you sell the cars.'

George reached into his mouth, pulled out a full set of dentures and studied them. 'Look. What if I can give you something to tide you over.' It wasn't easy understanding what he was saying with his teeth out. He slurred and spat his words.

'How much?' Jed asked.

'Five hundred. Each.'

'Five hundred! You promised us five thousand dollars all up for that car. We drove it into the yard and you rubbed your hands together like it was gold. That was your exact words, George. *Gold!* Fuck it. This isn't fair.'

'Hey!' George snarled. He put his teeth back in, to be sure his next comment was clearly understood. 'Don't you be swearing at me. You're only a kid and I'm a fucking businessman. Show some respect. I've got a local Jack in my pocket, son. You behave or you'll find yourself in a lot of trouble.' George picked up a large monkey wrench from the table and directed it towards Jed. 'Now fucken settle down. Let me think what I can do for you.' He dropped the wrench and scratched the side of his head with one hand and his balls with the other. 'All right. Listen up. The best I can offer today is one thousand. On top of that, you bring me another car. I don't care what it is, as long as it's in decent order. You do that and I'll spot you another two grand on delivery. It's a good deal.'

'And we still have a contract on the Mercedes?' Jed asked.

'As soon as it's shifted, I'll pay you what's owed on that as well.' He dropped the wrench on the table. 'So, we have a deal?'

'Almost,' Jed said. 'You pay us two thousand deposit now, not one thousand, and we have a deal.'

George nodded his head. 'Good.' He fiddled with the combination of the safe he kept under the desk, opened the door, counted two thousand dollars in grubby notes and handed them to Jed.

'When can you deliver?'

'Saturday night.'

'Okay. I'll leave the gates unlocked.'

The following Saturday, around one in the morning, Dominic sat perched on a boulder overlooking the country club car park. Jed lay on his back in the damp grass enjoying his third joint of the night. He was smoking it on the back of the half a dozen beers he'd downed earlier and a couple of unidentifiable blue tablets handed to him by the doorman out front of the *Motorhead*, a vacant warehouse that passed for the town's only nightclub.

Dominic ran an eye over the line of cars. Not one of them had a dent or cracked windscreen. 'Where do you reckon they get all the money for these cars?'

'My guess would be that most of them are lawyers, coppers or criminals. Take your pick.' Jed took a drag on his joint and held the smoke deep in his lungs. 'Drugs. It's where all the big money is. Maybe we should give it a go. We deliver this second car maybe we could pool our earnings. Four grand would buy us a decent purse of tablets. We could sell them around town and double our earnings.'

Dominic had no interest in selling drugs, and little more in stealing cars, he realised, surveying the car park.

Jed got to his knees, fell forward onto his face, and giggled.

'You sure you're okay to drive?' Dominic asked.

'I'm good to go. I always have a beer and some weed before a job. Eases me into the work. Pat was the same. Dunno why, but I can get nervous behind the wheel. You remember driver education back at school? *Safety first,* he giggled again. He gave up the effort of trying to get to his feet, lay on his back and looked up at the clear night sky. The stars shone from one side of a dark blanket to the other, and a full moon floated above the mountain range in the distance.

'You do any of that astronomy shit at school? Looking up at the sky?' Jed asked.

'Next year. Mr Macleod takes a class out camping in the hills with this telescope he's got. It's like a cannon.'

'I know. I've been up there with him. Me and Pat. He ever talk to you about it? You know he was mad for the stars Pat was.'

The news surprised Dominic. 'Pat never mentioned any stars to me.'

Jed raised his arm in the air, extended a finger and waved it across the sky.

'Well, he liked the stars almost as much as he did cars. Problem is, you can't steal a star. He knew the names of every one of them. This might sound dumb, but Pat decided we should pick a star each and name it after ourselves. You too. He named a star after his little brother.'

'Really?'

'Yeah. Really. Don't know which one is which now. Our stars. Most of them look the same. But I know this one.' He pointed to a bright star low in the eastern sky. 'You see that one way over there on its own winking at us?'

'Yeah. I see it.'

'Well, Macleod, he aimed his telescope at that star, lined us up and got us to take a look at it.'

Jed sat up, wiped his mouth and straightened his back, as if he was about to make an important announcement. 'And you know what he told us?'

Dominic wasn't paying attention. He was thinking Jed was in no state to break into and steal a car, let alone drive it back to Barron's yard.

'You listening to me, Dom? You know what he told us?'

'What did he tell you?'

'I know this might sound crazy, but the star we were looking at that night, the same star you can see up there winking at you now, it's dead. Fucken dead.'

'Dead?'

'Yep. And it's been dead for a million years. Maybe longer than that. The light you can see up there, it's taken all that time to get here. Right now that star, where the light is coming from, it's already dead.'

Dominic looked up at the star, burning bright yellow at the centre with exploding orange dust at its edge.

'A star as bright as that one, I don't see how it could die. It has to be alive.' He jumped from the boulder. 'Too bad Pat didn't love the stars a little more.'

'What's that fucken mean?'

'It would have been a lot better for my mum and dad and me, for all of us, if Pat had got more out of looking through a telescope at the stars than he did driving cars.' He began walking away. 'I'm going to sort this out.'

'Where you going?' Jed yelled. 'We got this job to do. One car and it's the jackpot.'

Jed dropped his pants and pissed in the dirt, throwing his head back and staring up at the sky. His eyes filled with tears and the stars blurred. By the time he'd zipped his jeans, Dominic was on the other side of the open field behind the country club, taking a shortcut through the bush, heading for the scrap yard. Jed stumbled after him calling, 'What about the car?'

Around two that morning Dominic Cross was perched high in a memorial tree on the side of the highway, the same one that had killed his brother. The scent of petrol filled the air. A burning Mercedes two-door sedan parked in the rear of George Barron's scrap yard had turned the night sky blood red. Jed lay at the base of the tree, sleeping. When the Mercedes exploded, shattering the windows of a row of cars parked nearby, he woke up. A second car quickly caught fire. Then another. Jed got to his feet and looked up, in search of the death star. The sky appeared to be on fire. He looked over to Dominic.

'What do we do now?'

'What do you mean?'

'Well, our money, what's owed us, you just blew it up. And you've probably sent George Barron broke. Somehow, I don't reckon he'd be insured.'

Dominic said nothing. He and Jed walked along the highway towards town. They went their separate ways at the railway crossing. The passenger train hadn't run for years and the only goods train passed through the town once a week without stopping. Rather than return home, Dominic walked on to the cemetery. Pat had been buried alongside his grandparents. The grave was marked with a mound of clay. The floral wreaths and bouquets that had been placed on top had dried and faded.

Dominic stood at the foot of his brother's grave, unsure of what to do. He had no inclination to recite a prayer. He dug his hand into the earth, scooped up a handful of clay and turned away. As he walked home he kneaded the clay in his hand until he'd created a rounded ball. He stopped in front of the family home, tossing the ball from one hand to the other before pitching it into the morning sky.

JOE ROBERTS

JOE ROBERTS WOKE EARLY, ON HIS BACK, his arms folded across his chest. He resembled a corpse prepared for a funeral. Turning onto his side he felt a pain above his hip bone. He'd been experiencing discomfort for weeks but in recent days the pain had gotten worse. He had started to feel an additional stabbing pain when he moved too quickly. Joe turned his head and looked over to the window, a sliver of light radiating from the streetlight outside. He slowly rolled over and checked the time. The clock sat on the bedside table slightly obscured by an open packet of painkillers. The time, just after four in the morning, caught him by surprise. He never used an alarm, had a knack of waking up ten minutes before he needed to, whatever the hour. He would have preferred to lay in bed but had no choice, his bladder about to burst.

The letter the hospital had mailed to him contained a clear set of instructions, written in capital letters. Most importantly, he was required to fast from midnight on the night before the procedure. He'd also been ordered to drink a *minimum* of two litres of water in the hours before bed to ensure his kidneys were flushed clean. Joe hadn't realised it would take such effort to get the water down until he was sipping his fourth glass of the evening.

He involuntarily grabbed his side as he sat up, swivelled and placed the soles of his feet on the carpeted floor. He stood and hobbled towards the bathroom cradling his stomach the way a heavily pregnant woman might do. As he took a slow, intermittent piss, and inspected the toilet bowl, the pain gradually eased. There was no blood in his urine, a good sign at least, he thought. He flushed the toilet and scrubbed his hands vigorously, a lifelong habit, before gingerly climbing back into bed and resting his head on the pillow. He spent the next hour looking over at the clock every few minutes before finally drifting off.

At a quarter past six – fifteen minutes *after* he'd planned to be up – Joe woke with a fright, drenched in sweat. He pressed the palms of both hands against his chest as if he were trying to stop his heart exploding in his rib cage. He felt a chill in his back, awkwardly removed his damp pyjama top and let it fall to the floor. He forced himself to remain still as he concentrated on regulating his breathing. Eventually, he felt calm enough to get out of bed.

Clutching the box of painkillers, he went into the bathroom, turned on the light, leaned over the sink and studied his face in the mirror. He took four pills out of the box and swallowed them with a glass of water. He could hear the woman in the flat below singing in the shower. It was the same tune each morning. The song was French and although Joe didn't understand more than a few words, it sounded sad against his ear. He often heard the woman singing as he ate his breakfast, or a little later saying goodbye to her son before she left for work. Joe sometimes passed her on the stairway carrying heavy bags of shopping from the market. The woman had dark skin and wore printed dresses with colourful scarves. The boy was sometimes with her, trailing in her shadow.

Having showered and shaved Joe returned to the bedroom with a towel around his waist. The room was cold and his skin was goosebumped. He couldn't decide what to wear to the hospital and was annoyed by his indecision, a condition that seemed to accompany the pain he'd been experiencing. He laid a dark suit out on the bed, then a pair of black pants and a casual jacket. Although he never set out to impress, he liked to dress well. Joe had spent his childhood in a Boys Home wearing anonymous hand-me-downs. On special occasions, such as a visit to the Home by a government minister or prospective donor, the boys were provided with a clean white shirt and marched around the quadrangle before lining up for inspection.

Regardless of the painful memories associated with it, Joe felt oddly *clean* in a white shirt. He took one from the wardrobe and slipped it on, followed by the black pants. He put on a pair of black socks and highly polished black leather shoes and examined himself in the full-length mirror on the back of the wardrobe door. Satisfied, he went into the kitchen, turned on the radio and made himself a cup of black tea, itself a prohibited substance that morning. He sat at a narrow wooden table, opened a large envelope, and again read over the information regarding his procedure.

The woman from the flat below called to her son, '*Au revoir.*' Joe heard the door close as she left the building. The hospital letter reminded him he would need to provide 'proof of birth'. He went into the hallway, opened the closet door and retrieved a wooden box. He stood in the hallway for a minute or two, unwilling to move, regarding the box as if it were a delicate object. Back at the kitchen table, he opened the lid and read the inscription carved into the timber – *J. R. 1969*. He pulled out the birth certificate and studied it closely, in search of a mystery never to be solved. The birthdate, 29 March 1957, had been registered at the same hospital he was to attend that morning. The name of the *Mother* had been crudely blacked-out in smudged ink. Joe ran a fingertip lightly over the mark, a ritual he'd repeated many times. On the line below was the word *Father.* And on the dotted line alongside of it, scripted in a neat, flowing hand was the word *Unknown.* Like most boys in the Home, having no knowledge of his father's identity, Joe had invented not only exotic names and identities for the *Unknown*, but a life of heroic adventure. It was not until many years later that he accepted no hero would be coming to rescue him, and that at least a blank space on a government document provided certainty. He folded the certificate and put it in the pocket of his suit jacket.

A tapping sound called to Joe from the window overlooking the front landing. He saw a cat sitting on the ledge. It had a black coat and white front paws. Joe kept one eye on the cat as he rinsed and dried his tea cup and returned it to the cupboard. He walked across to the window and leaned forward. Joe and the cat were separated by a sheet of glass. The cat leaned its head to one side and meowed at him. It tapped a paw on the glass. Joe tapped back with a fingernail and ordered the cat to *shoo!* The cat refused to budge and knocked at the glass with its paw. Joe knocked back, a little heavier. The cat arched its back, hissed angrily, dropped from the ledge and disappeared from sight.

Joe put his jacket on, picked up his keys and wallet from a glass bowl on the kitchen bench, left the flat and locked the front door behind him. He heard a *meow* and looked down. The pesky cat was sitting at his feet. It stood up, arched its back and rubbed the side of its body up against his leg.

Joe clapped his hands together. 'You lost or something?'

He paused at the stairway and turned back. The cat was making itself comfortable on his doormat. On the ground floor he saw the boy from the flat below, his face resting against the window looking onto the street. As Joe passed by he could feel the boy watching him closely, just as the cat had done. He had already turned his back and was walking along the pathway to the footbridge, when the boy raised his hand and waved.

Joe didn't particularly like cats, but as he walked across the street he worried over the stray, concerned that it may not have any food to eat. He also began to worry about the boy. He wondered if the mother made breakfast for the boy, or if he prepared it himself after she'd gone off to work. Maybe he didn't eat breakfast at all? The boy's welfare was none of his concern, and Joe wasn't one to meddle, and yet he couldn't get the image of the child at the window out of his head.

It had been raining overnight and the emptied clouds had left behind a flattened grey sky. Joe walked along the footbridge over the freeway. The morning traffic, floating in a haze of fumes, was already at a standstill. Joe looked at the sculpture hovering above the freeway, a line of narrow obelisks, painted blood red, leaning precariously over the traffic. Birds wove a path through the sculpture, enjoying the morning exercise of gliding loops. At its base a collection of debris in a pond – plastic bottles, food wrappings, three overturned shopping trolleys, a deflated beach ball. Joe sniffed the stagnant air and walked on to the railway station.

The platform was deserted. Joe checked his watch. The next train, due in three minutes, failed to arrive ten minutes later. Joe stood on the yellow line separating himself from the tracks. He leaned forward and searched the line. It was empty. He heard a barking cough and was shocked to see a teenage girl stagger from the shadows of the waiting room. She wore a short denim skirt and black singlet decorated with sequins. A pair of high-heeled shoes dangled in one hand. The heel of one shoe had snapped off. The girl had a tattoo above one breast, a pair of dice, a five and a two. She had cuts and bruises on both arms and the front of her skirt was smeared with mud. She lunged at Joe with an open hand. He noticed she had several broken fingernails. He stepped away and looked from her bleached-blonde hair to her pained face. She froze, leaned forward with an outstretched arm and mouthed a word that stuck in her throat.

A train whistled in the distance and a cold wind cut across the platform. Joe turned up the collar of his jacket and watched the dull yellow eye of the train rounding the bend in the distance. The train arrived and the automatic doors opened.

The carriage was warm. Joe found a seat opposite a young man wearing a cheap suit, scuffed leather shoes and earphones. He was drumming a beat against his thighs with open hands.

'Junky,' the passenger opposite shouted, not bothering to remove his earphones. He raised a finger towards the girl outside. 'Hey, piss off, you scrag!' When she didn't move he took out his earphones and banged on the glass. 'Piss off!' The young man laughed and leaned across to Joe. 'Fucken junky. You see her arms? She's on the gear.'

Joe ignored him and stared out the window, feigning interest in the rusting iron roofs of houses, ramshackle backyards and vegetable plots.

'She'd be on the fucken job, too,' the passenger continued, loud enough for the whole carriage to hear. 'That's how they pay for it. The gear. Hawk the fork.' He smiled and looked around. Realising that nobody was listening, he sneered, stuck the earbuds back in his ears and returned to the drum solo.

Joe stood on the street corner in front of the hospital entrance, a deafening sound in the sky overhead. A helicopter hovered above the building for several seconds before turning and flying towards the city centre. He took the referral letter out of his jacket pocket and read through it a final time. He looked anxiously over his shoulder towards the intersection and back to the automatic glass doors leading into the foyer.

Walking through the doors he passed a florist and a post office, manoeuvring his way through the crowd to the lift. He rode to the fourth floor and, seeing a blue line etched into the tiles, followed it around several corners and along a long narrow corridor until he arrived at the radiology clinic. The large reception room was full mostly of men around Joe's age or older. He handed the letter to a woman seated behind a desk. She scratched the tip of her nose with a ball-point pen as she read the letter. She looked over the top of her glasses at Joe.

'Good morning, Mr Roberts. You need to fill out this form.' She handed Joe the pen and a sheet of paper attached to a clipboard. 'Please complete the details and hand the form to the specialist when your name is called.'

'Where should I ...'

'Wherever you can find a seat.'

Joe found a vacant chair in the far corner of the room, sat down and began filling out the form. He stopped writing each time a name was called over a speaker above his head. He heard someone reciting the Lord's Prayer and became distracted. Looking around he noticed one of the few young people in the room, a woman around the age of twenty. She was holding the hand of an older woman who was clutching a set of rosary beads and rocking slightly as she prayed.

A name was called: *Ms Catani to cubicle three.* The younger woman stood and straightened her dress. The older woman, silent now, stood with deliberate slowness and kissed the younger woman on the forehead, watching closely as the girl walked across the room towards an open door.

Joe completed his form and stuck the clipboard under his arm. He looked across at a couple sitting opposite. The husband wore a pair of grey pants and a flannelette chequered shirt under a hand-knitted vest. Lumps of dried clay were stuck to the soles of his work boots. He looked like he'd just strolled out of a suburban vegetable patch. Speaking animatedly to each other, the couple's conversation shifted from English to Italian and something in between. The woman smiled at her husband from time to time, leaning into him with her heavy body. She whispered in his ear. He laughed and she slapped him playfully on the arm before resting her head on his shoulder.

Another name was called and the couple got to their feet, he tucking the tail of his shirt into his pants and, with his wife's help, walking to a cubicle. They waddled side by side in harmony. A thin, balding doctor waited for them with an open hand. As the old man walked into the cubicle his wife massaged the small of his back with an open palm.

Eventually, Joe was called. *Mr Joseph Roberts. To cubicle four.*

Joe stood up too quickly and felt a stab of pain in his side. He was surprised to see a female doctor waiting in the doorway; a slim woman with dark hair tied into a bun. She offered her hand. 'Joseph, I'm Doctor McGee. I'll be taking care of you today,' she said in an accent that Joe thought was most likely Scottish. She ushered him into a small room, closed the door and asked him to take a seat. She placed a second chair opposite and sat down, close enough to make Joe feel uncomfortable. He could smell her perfume. The scent of orange. She was holding a manila file with his name written on the front in heavy black pen. She quickly read through the file, occasionally nodding her head and sighing.

The doctor looked up. 'The urinary bleed that you experienced three weeks ago, can you tell me something more about it, Joseph?'

Joe shifted in his chair. He wasn't sure what to say.

The doctor prompted him. 'Can you begin by telling me what time of the day it was?'

'Well … I must have got out of bed at around one in the morning, needing to go to the toilet. And when I did, well … I was bleeding.'

'And when had you last gone to the toilet before that, for a wee?'

Joe wasn't sure and took a guess. 'Most likely before I got into bed for the night. Maybe around ten o'clock.'

'And there was no blood in your urine?'

'None.'

'Are you sure?' she asked, leaning forward. The doctor was close enough for Joe to notice a blood spot in one of her hazel-coloured pupils.

'I'm sure,' he said. 'I would have noticed.'

She smiled with satisfaction. 'Good. Now tell me about the colour of the urine. How would you describe it?'

Joe didn't know how to best answer the question. 'The colour? It was, you know, like blood. It was red.'

'Yes. I'm sure it was, Joseph. It would have been *reddish* in colour, but I need to consider the amount of blood in your urine. A more accurate description of the colour will help. This may sound odd, but let's imagine that your urine was a wine. If so, would you describe it as a claret? A darker red. Or would it be more the colour of a rosé, lighter, even pink in colour?'

Joseph thought about the question and remembered that at the time he was convinced he was peeing straight blood.

'It was a darker red. More like a claret.'

The doctor tapped him lightly on the knee, as she might do to a well-behaved child. 'Very good.' She wrote a few comments in his file. 'Thank you, Joseph. Now, tell me, have you had another bleed since you came into Casualty that first morning?'

'Twice more. The same day, while I was in here. There was nothing more until I had another bleed two days ago.'

'Two days ago. Was it the same dark colour as the first bleed?'

'Yes. The same.'

'And when you wee, particularly when you have had the bleeds, has there been pain?'

'Not when I go to the toilet. But when I wake in the night wanting to go, yes. And I have this other pain in my side sometimes, mostly when I move too quickly.'

Joe hadn't expected he would be required to answer so many questions. Each time she asked a question the doctor moved a little closer. Eventually he could feel her breath on his cheek. He began to involuntarily massage his stomach. The doctor, sensing his anxiety, stood up and moved across to a narrow examination table covered with a fresh white sheet.

'In cases such as this,' she explained, 'and in consideration of your age, we're going to put you through a series of examinations, commencing today with a full body scan. I want to get some nice pictures of your organs, Joseph. Your kidneys in particular. It's important that we find out what is causing this bleeding. Each examination we put you through will help to build a diagnosis, largely through a process of elimination.' She patted the white sheet with the palm of her hand. 'But first up I need to go over you myself,' she said, pulling a two-step wooden ladder out from under the table. 'I'll need you to undress and pop up here for me.'

'Pardon?' Joe replied.

'I need you to take your clothing off, Joseph, so that I can examine you.'

'My clothing?'

'Yes. Down to your underwear please.'

Joseph slowly removed his jacket and shirt. He sat back down on the chair, took off his shoes and socks and stood again, to attention.

'And your trousers.'

Joe unbuckled his belt, dropped his pants and stepped out of them. Reduced to his underpants and singlet, he climbed onto the table and folded his arms across his chest like a shy boy. As the doctor checked his blood pressure and heart rate Joe concentrated on a *Life for Living Advice* poster on the wall. The doctor lifted Joe's singlet and had the stethoscope pressed to the left side of his chest when she noticed a series of small circular raised scars under his left breast, between his two lower ribs. She looked more closely at the scars and ran a gloved hand across the areas of raised skin. Joe twitched involuntarily.

'I'm sorry, Joseph. But what do we have here? I've seen burn scars similar to these before. Cigarettes would be my guess?'

Joe continued studying the poster. The doctor gently prodded the scar tissue.

'Yes. I'd say these are burns, Joseph. A long time ago. Would I be right?'

'Yes,' Joe sighed. 'Many years ago.' He could not curb his curiosity. 'How can you tell?'

'Because I'm a doctor,' she laughed, attempting to ease the tension. 'Before coming to work in Australia I spent two years with *Médecins Sans Frontières*. Doctors Without Borders. Have you heard of them?'

'No.'

'We work in sites of disaster. Floods and earthquakes. War zones. Any place there's a need for us.' She rested an open palm against Joseph's chest. 'You know, there are so many ways to damage the human body,' she said, in an oddly cheerful voice. 'Guns. Grenades. Machetes. You name it. Oh yes. And let's not forget torture,' she smiled. 'Regardless of new technologies one of the common weapons of choice remains the good old Marlboro filter tip using human skin as an ashtray. Or the tip of a metal stake heated on a fire. Simple and cheap. And a method that gets the job done. Apparently.'

The doctor dug into her jacket pocket and came out with a pencil-sized silver torch. She shone the beam over the scars, examining them closely, and let out a soft laugh. 'Looks like the planets of the solar system lined up here. This was done with a sense of order in mind. How and when did you come by these injuries, Joseph?'

He hesitated before answering. 'It was long ago,' he shrugged. 'I really can't remember.'

The doctor raised an eyebrow, unimpressed.

Joe did some quick arithmetic in his head. 'It would have to be close to fifty years.'

The odd smile left her face. She looked down at the clipboard. 'Fifty years back. You were just a boy, Joseph.'

Joe stood up and reached for his clothes. 'I'm sorry, but I

thought we were here so you could help me out with the bleeding? This other stuff, it doesn't matter. It was so long back, I can't remember much about it. And it's got nothing to do with how I'm feeling now.'

'Let me share something with you, Joseph. We try to forget the truth sometimes. All of us, walking in and out of this hospital. Me as much as anyone. But the body, it never lies. It carries our scars, on the inside and outside. The body never forgets.' She put a hand on Joe's shoulder. 'Is there anything more you can tell me?'

'As I said, there's nothing,' Joe answered forcefully, but in no way convincingly.

She leaned against the examination table and watched closely as Joe methodically put his shoes on and tied the laces.

'Reading your notes, you were transferred at school age from a government to a religious institution?'

'That's right,' Joe answered, feigning calmness. 'The Christian Brothers. I was with them until I was sixteen.'

'Do you know if they have medical records for you, Joseph?'

'I really don't know,' Joe answered, honestly.

The doctor peeled off her gloves, took a fresh pair out of a box on her desk and put them on. She studied the tip of a gloved finger as she spoke. 'Now that we've finished here, you'll be having another examination this morning, just along the corridor. If your kidneys or bladder are not the culprit, we'll follow up in a week.'

'Why do you look at the bladder?' Joe asked.

'We'll be ruling out cancer.'

She detected a slight twitch on Joe's face.

'Please don't worry too much, Joseph. In your case bladder

cancer is the least likely diagnosis. But as with any urinary bleed, we must get inside the bladder and take some pictures to rule it out.'

She raised a long and shapely index finger in the air and smiled sympathetically at Joe. 'But test number one, unfortunately, is your prostate.'

Joe left the cubicle and once again followed the blue line on the tiled floor down the corridor where he was met by a nurse who handed him a white hospital gown and a large plastic-lined brown paper bag. She directed Joe to a changing room, with the stern order to *remove everything, including jewels and dentures.* Joe took his clothes off for the second time that day, put the gown on and placed his clothes in the paper bag. He sat down on a bench with two other men also cradling their possessions. One of them was the older man he'd seen earlier in the waiting room with his wife. The man nodded and smiled at Joe, who smiled sheepishly back. Not long after, a fourth patient exited the changing cubicle. He dropped his paper bag and quickly managed to work himself into a frenzy, trying to fasten the ties at the back of the gown. Joe couldn't help but smile, suddenly remembering the grainy black and white film footage he'd once seen of the famous magician, Houdini, hanging upside down from a chain above a river, attempting to wriggle his way out of a straitjacket.

The old man started to laugh and the others joined in, including the patient wrestling with his gown. The old man got to his feet and clapped his hands together.

'*Guardami.* Watch me.'

He theatrically demonstrated a dressing technique he'd obviously perfected earlier. He lifted his arms above his head and slipped them out of the short sleeves of the gown. He then grabbed at the neck of the gown and turned the ties to the front. He untied them, exposing the white hairs on his chest, his decent belly, and a penis he saw only in the mirror of a morning. While Joe looked away, a little embarrassed, the man concentrated on the task at hand.

'*Questo è il modo per farlo,*' he smiled, re-doing the ties and manoeuvring the gown around his body until the ties had returned to the back. With all four men properly attired they sat and smiled at each other, occasionally laughing quietly. One by one they were escorted into another room until eventually Joe was alone. The room was cold. He looked down at his toes. They were slowly changing colour, from pink to blue. He draped an arm across his stomach and tentatively fingered each of the small circular scars on his left ribs. He'd forgotten nothing about what had caused the scars, and he was sure the doctor knew as much. In fact, once prodded by the doctor's questioning, the details of the many occasions he'd spent in agony came flooding back to him. He sniffed the air, sure he could smell burning flesh.

'Mr Roberts?'

A nurse stood waiting. Although Joe had managed to tie his gown properly, he reached a hand around his back and grabbed at the draughty opening.

The nurse winked at him and smiled. 'Good morning, handsome. I'm your date for the day.'

She took Joe by one arm and escorted him into an operating theatre dominated by machines and monitors attached by a weave of electrical cables and wiring. Joe quickly counted at least half a dozen staff, each wearing a light blue uniform. The nurse guided Joe to a long narrow table and eased him onto his back. She handed him a pair of sunglasses before switching on a bright light above the table.

'If you have any concerns, Joseph, then you're most welcome to hold my hand. But I have to let you know, I don't kiss on a first date, even for a fella as good looking as you.' She reached for his hand and squeezed it. 'But if you behave yourself, I will let you take me dancing next week.' She winked at him a second time and placed a tourniquet on his lower left arm.

Joe felt a cold sensation on his skin, above his wrist. 'This may hurt a smidge,' the nurse said. He felt helpless. A needle went into his arm. He could hear the quiet humming of the machines and one of the staff talking about an opera he'd seen the night before. The man walked over to the table and stood reading Joe's medical notes. He then placed a hand gently on Joe's chest.

'Good morning, Mr Roberts. I'm Mr Lee, your specialist. Let me explain what will be happening this morning. And if you are uncertain at all, if you have any questions for me, please ask. We have just inserted a catheter into your arm. In a moment we'll inject a substance into the catheter which will help us get a good picture of your kidneys. You'll most likely experience an odd taste in your mouth, as if you're biting on metal. And after a few seconds there will be another sensation, a feeling that you're wetting yourself.'

He lifted his hand for a moment then allowed it to return to Joe's chest.

'But don't worry. It is only a sensation. It's nothing to be concerned about.' The doctor turned and nodded at the nurse. 'You're in the best of hands. Do you have any questions?'

'No.'

The feelings were exactly as the doctor had described them. Within thirty seconds of the chemicals entering his bloodstream Joe felt the taste of metal in his mouth, and a few seconds later he was sure he was peeing himself. The nurse noticed the worried look on his face and gripped his hand.

'It's okay, Joseph. It's only a trick played on your mind by the drugs. You rest easy and let me take care of you.'

Following the scan Joe was sent back to the changing room where he was told to dress, return to the original waiting room and arrange his next appointment. As he was about to slip his white shirt on he noticed his scarred upper body in the mirror. He lifted an arm and looked closely at the old burns for the first time in many years. The doctor had been right, he thought. *The body never lies.*

Joe finished dressing but once out of the change room somehow made a wrong turn, following the purple line instead of the blue one. He opened a glass door into a room dominated by brightly painted walls with numbers, letters and stencils of farm animals. The room was full of young children. Some were quietly playing. Others were squealing with joy, chasing each other around the room. A few, who were clearly unwell, did not move. A young girl, who could not have been more than three or four years old, ran across the room to Joe. She stopped in front of him, smiled and offered him a toy, a cloth doll with plaited hair and a candy-striped dress. The doll had a tear drawn on its face.

'She has all my hair,' the girl said.

Joe looked down at the girl's pale skin and the wisps of fine hair on top of an otherwise bald head. The girl's mother called to her and the girl turned and walked slowly across the room, holding the rag doll to her chest.

Joe retraced his steps back to the waiting room. He sat down on a bench and closed his eyes. A few minutes later he was shaken by the receptionist.

'You look worn out, Mr Roberts. Next time you should bring someone along with you. It really does help.'

She offered Joe a pen and pointed to a blank line on the admissions sheet. 'You never filled this out. *Next of Kin*. We need the contact number for a family member.'

Joe looked up at the woman, confused. She could have been speaking a foreign language. Finally, realising what she was asking, he was too worn out to evade the question. 'I don't have any family,' he answered, shrugging his shoulders.

'Well, we still need a name. A friend?'

Joe looked down at his black leather shoes, annoyed that one toe was scuffed. 'There's no one to contact.' He gathered himself and stood up. 'Is this really necessary?' he asked, raising his voice and surprising both the receptionist and himself with his tone.

'Okay. That's fine, Mr Roberts. Let's organise your next appointment.'

She handed him a pink slip of paper. 'There you are, Mr Roberts. We will see you next week. It might be a good idea to also mark the appointment on a calendar. It helps.'

Joe took the slip. 'I'm sorry,' he said.

'Sorry for what?' She seemed genuinely puzzled.

'I raised my voice to you just now. I'm sorry. It's been a tiring day.'

She left her desk and walked to where Joseph was standing. She took hold of his hand. 'This can be tough going. I know, Joseph. I've been on both sides of this counter. Whatever happens, we stick with our patients, all the way.' She kissed him on the cheek. 'Now don't tell anyone I was nice to you. I'm supposed to be the hard one around here. We'll see you next week.'

By the time Joe arrived home it was close to dark. The wind had picked up. He wondered if it was about to rain. He could see the boy from the flat below sitting on his doorstep. Joe was surprised. He'd occasionally seen the boy walking to and from school on his own, but he never played in the street or hung around the landing.

'What are you doing out here?' Joe asked.

He'd not been around young boys since he was a teenager, and was unaware of his brusqueness, which appeared to have startled the boy. 'Is there something wrong?' he asked, a little more gently.

'I'm locked out of my flat,' he answered, pointing at the door.

Joe stared at the door, as if it might offer an explanation. 'Is your mother not at home?'

The boy shook his head from side to side.

'Do you know where she is?'

The boy looked up at Joe. 'She's working. At her job in the factory.'

Joe was puzzled as to why the boy would be left in the street on his own. 'Does she know you're out here?'

'No. I lost my key and don't know where it is.'

Joe wasn't sure what to do. 'What time do you expect that she'll be home?'

The boy shrugged. 'Most days she's here when I get home. But on Wednesdays, today, she works late. She already cooked my dinner for me, last night. It's ready to eat.'

The boy was clearly distressed. Joe sunk his hands in his pockets and began nervously tapping the toe of his shoe as he thought about what he could do to help.

'Are you hungry?' Joe asked

The boy nodded his head. 'Yes'.

'My name is Joe. You are?'

The boy hesitated before answering. 'I'm Charles.'

'Okay, Charles. If you want to come upstairs, I can make some spaghetti for us to eat and you can wait with me until your mother comes home.'

Charles vigorously shook his head from side to side. 'No, thank you.'

'Why?'

'Because I'm not allowed to go with people I don't know.'

'Oh.' Joe felt the pain in his side. 'Well, that's good advice. I'm not good with strangers either. Let's see. What about if you wait here and I bring you a bowl of spaghetti? Would that be okay?'

Charles smiled, slightly. 'I think so.'

'Good. First let me get you a rug, so you don't get cold before we eat. And then we can have some pasta down here on the landing.'

Joe boiled water on the stove, opened a container of pasta sauce and grated some cheese. He went out onto the landing several times and looked over the balcony but could not see the boy. When the spaghetti was ready he left the flat with a bowl in each hand and two spoons and forks in his back pocket. Charles was sitting on his doorstep waiting, with Joe's rug wrapped around his legs.

'Here you are,' Joe said. 'I learned to cook this for forty boys when I wasn't a lot older than you.' He handed Charles a bowl and they ate together in silence.

'What do you think?' Joe asked after Charles had finished, leaving a small amount of pasta in the bowl.

'It's good. Thank you,' he said, politely. 'Do you have any friends who live near here?' he asked.

If Joe had been honest he would have told Charles that he had no friends. He decided against saying so. 'They live somewhere else. In their own houses. What about you? Where do your friends live?'

Charles gave the question serious thought. 'I play football with some boys, but they're not my friends. They are only boys from school.'

The comment made perfect sense to Joe. He'd seen many boys pass through the Home, but made friends with none of them. As he took the bowl from Charles, he heard a cat's meow and turned. The black cat with white socks jumped from a shrub edging the landing. A long silky cobweb hung from one ear. The cat sniffed the air.

'I think this cat is hungry,' Joe said. He placed Charles's bowl on the ground and pushed it towards the cat. 'You want some, kitty?'

The cat backed away, sniffed the air, walked forward, stuck its face in the bowl and began eating, ferociously.

'Do you like cats, Charles?'

'I like them, but I've never had a cat of my own.'

'Me either,' Joe said. 'They know how to look after themselves. That's a good thing. It's the cat that decides if it wants to be friends, not the other way around.'

Charles sighed. 'I think my mother will be here soon.'

The cat finished the pasta and licked the bowl.

'Would you like me to sit here with you while you wait?' Joe asked. 'I don't mind.'

'If you like, yes.'

They watched as the black cat turned away from them and disappeared into the garden.

THE WHITE GIRL

I FELL IN LOVE WITH HEATHER MORAN the first time I saw her, on the morning I fronted up to school in a pair of piss-stained shorts. She wore a clean dress. I was eleven years old and no other kids would let me sit next to them on account of the bad smell. Riding my bone-shaker bike to school along a two-mile dirt road I was so scared of being late, which I was most mornings, and earning the strap for my trouble, I pissed my pants rather than stop and take a leak behind a tree.

Most of the kids in class laughed and teased me and I hid down the back of the room, trying my best to wipe the tears from my dirty face with one hand and making a fist with the other. I wanted to slam that fist into someone's face, and didn't care whose it was, as long as I caused some pain and drew blood. Mr Wrench, our teacher, marched into the room, banged his books down on his desk, stared at me through his coke-bottle specs and pointed a bony finger in my direction.

'Sexton, find yourself a seat. And not on your own. If you prefer solitary confinement I can call the constable and have you hauled off. You can join your delinquent older brother.'

The class giggled like a mad choir. I searched the centre aisle for a place to sit. Any kid with a spare seat moved their arse to the middle of the bench and spread out, letting it be known there was no place for me.

Heather was the new girl. She got up, walked to the back of the room, tugged at my T-shirt and pointed to her desk.

'You can sit next to me, if you like,' she whispered. 'My name is Heather.'

The other girls in the class looked at her in disgust, like she'd asked me to put a hand in her pants for a play.

I shuffled behind her and sat down, as close as I could to the end of the bench without falling off. I didn't want her passing out on account of the stink. I sniffed the air to get a whiff of myself, but all I could smell was something like *Velvet* soap coming from her golden plaited hair.

She sat back, looking at the blackboard, paying attention to old Wrench. I took a good peep at her. She had to be the cleanest person I'd ever seen. Her dress had no stains or repair work, and there were no marks on her fair-skinned arms except for some freckles. No insect bites or old scars like I had.

Wrench's stick of chalk scratched the board as he wrote up the lesson and the swinging heels of school boots scraped against the floorboards. I listened closely to Heather breathing quietly in and out, and decided right there and then that I was in love with her. I'd never loved anyone before, except for Angie, and she didn't count, she was just a wild cat that had befriended me three years back after I threw her a chicken carcass in the side yard.

At lunchtime I took up my usual spot, under the peppercorn tree in the far corner of the schoolyard, trying hard not to think about the hunger pains in my gut. Heather stood in the middle of the yard, the sun catching her hair. She smiled and walked towards me, holding a lunchbox under one arm. She stopped, opened the lid, took out a sandwich and held a half in each hand.

'Would you like some? It's Vegemite and cheese.'

I looked up at the thick slices of bread, knowing I could gulp the lot in one mouthful, even if the filling had been nothing more than dripping with pepper sprinkled on it for taste.

'Nup. It's not mine to have.'

She leaned forward and offered me the half sandwich anyway.

'Please take it. There's more here than I can eat.'

I took the sandwich and dirtied the white bread with my grubby fingers. Heather took two shining apples from the lunchbox and offered one to me.

'What's your name?' She smiled. Her teeth were straight as light posts and even whiter than her skin.

'Noah.'

'Noah who?'

'You a copper or something, with all the questions?'

She took a bite from her sandwich. 'I'm sorry. I won't ask another one. Are you going to eat your sandwich?'

'It's Sexton. Noah Sexton. Didn't you hear Wrench call out to me?'

'Why do you sit over here?' she asked.

I stared at the sandwich. I wanted to get a good look at it before taking a bite. 'You said there'd be no more questions. And you asked another two already'

'That was the last one. I promise.' She scratched the end of her nose.

'I sit over here because I'm a Sexton.'

My surname would normally be explanation enough. Being a newcomer, she didn't get it.

'What about it? That's just a name.'

'Not our name. We're cursed. Don't get too close to me. You can catch it, like a disease.'

'Don't be silly. I bet I can't catch anything from you.'

To prove her point she sat next to me, close enough that I could smell the sweet soap of her again.

'Can I ask you a question this time?'

She wiped crumbs from her dress. 'Of course.'

'What are you doing here?'

'Under this tree,' she laughed, but not like she was making fun of me.

'Nup. At this school? In this town?'

'My father is the new policeman. He's going to be in charge of the station. And my mother does a lot of work with the church.'

So she was a copper. Sort of.

Our mob was well known to the police, and I knew straightaway that as soon as her father got the story behind the family name, she wouldn't be sitting under any tree offering me Vegemite sandwiches.

My old man had been in and out of prison more times than

he'd had work. And most of my uncles, on both sides of the family, were no better. My older brother, Jeff, was two years into a seven-year sentence for armed robbery after taking up with a sawn-off shotgun. He was about to hit his third service station for the weekend when a passing squad car spotted him driving down the highway wearing his balaclava. They ran him off the road into a ditch.

Instead of wolfing the sandwich down like I would have done if I'd been on my own, I pretended I had a few manners, and took one bite at a time. After the sandwich I took a chomp of the apple. It tasted good. Sweet and juicy.

The air was a little too quiet. I guessed I needed to say something to show my gratitude.

'Do you have brothers and sisters?' I asked her.

'No. There's just my mother and father. What about you?'

'I have two older sisters, Dee and Jessie. They work in the butter factory, on the other side of town. And my brother, Jeff. He's … away.'

'Away where?'

I took another bite from the apple and chewed on it awhile. 'Just away.'

'Do you have any friends at school?'

'Nup. No friends no place. No one deals with us, 'cept the boys that come sniffing around for Dee and Jess. I don't look it as much as some, but we're Abos.'

She frowned.

'That's a dirty word. You shouldn't say that. My father was posted at an outstation in the desert before we moved here. People like you, we call them half-castes. It's more proper.'

'Well, round here it's not,' I laughed. 'An Abo's an Abo, no matter how black or white he is, my dad told us. Far as the whitefella is interested, shit smells just the same. My dad told us that, too.'

Heather wriggled around, less than comfortable about what I'd said. I didn't care too much. As pretty as she was, I was already thinking she was just another do-gooder. They came through town from time to time and then left when the place got too hard for them.

'What about the other Aboriginal families?' she asked. 'Are there others here?'

'We're the only mob left. One time there was more of us here than whitefellas. But like most places, more and more of them moved in until there was no room for us. The last of the big families took off more than two years back. They were Sextons too. Cousins on my old man's side. One of the boys, Stevie, was shot in the back when he got caught breaking into a farmer's toolshed one night. He was fourteen and skinny as a rake. His father, my uncle Claude, didn't have no money and had to bury him in a suitcase. Didn't matter how he was killed either. The law said the farmer was defending his family and his property. That was the end of it.'

'That's not fair.'

'Fair don't come into it. They're on top. Us on the bottom.'

'That won't happen with my dad. He's always fair, to both sides.'

I looked straight into Heather's big brown eyes. She believed what she was saying. The girl had plenty to learn.

'Where do you live, Noah?'

'In an old farmhouse out of town. The owner give up on it last drought. My grandpa, Teddy, was a roustabout for him, years back. Said we could stay in the house for nothing as long as we kept the grass down and the troublemakers out. We been there since, the house falling down around us, waiting for the land to be sold off.'

'It must be exciting, living on a farm. What animals do you have?'

'We got a milking cow that don't milk, hens too lazy to lay and a feral cat full of hate.'

'You said it was a farm. All farms have working animals.'

'Not this one. Fences've fallen down and the dam's dried up. If you want working animals, we got plenty of rats. A nest of them under the back verandah. And crows waiting to swoop from the trees and poke an eye out if you stand still long enough.'

Wrench walked out of the schoolroom and across the yard, which meant that it was time to head back to class. I stood up and dusted my pants off, for maybe the first time in my life. 'We have to get back,' I said. 'He goes mental anytime you're late in.'

Heather sat with me most lunchtimes after that day with a lunchbox loaded with sandwiches and homemade cakes. She said that once her mother had heard about me, and that I had no lunch of my own, she made a point of providing for two. The other kids in the class had started looking at Heather like she was trash.

Wrench called her aside after school one day and warned her off me.

'What did you say to him?'

'I told him that my mother was a Christian, I was a Christian, and that it was a sin to turn away from those in need.'

I didn't feel good being spoken of like a charity case. But I guess I was. And I was so in love with Heather by then I'd have put up with anything to sit close to her and share her food.

I took to scrubbing myself of a night with a cleaning brush, hard enough for the sharp bristles to draw blood. I hung my clothes on a line on the verandah overnight, giving the air a chance to work through them. In the morning I stuck my head under the cold tap in the kitchen and combed it through with the hairbrush my mum had left behind when she shot through.

Teddy, who'd be sitting at the table, concentrating on the steam coming out of the spout of the teapot, had worked out I was up to something.

'As far as I've heard you haven't been given a job on the carnivals, boy. It has to be a girl?'

'Shut up, will ya Teddy. Keep your eyes on the tea or you'll overbrew it and find yourself worked up with anger for the rest of the day.'

'Don't worry, I'm watching it. You got yourself a girl at school, Noah?'

I said nothing but he picked up the flush in my cheeks.

'They all white girls at that school. Don't be getting cocky and above yourself. Unless you want your nuts taken for a fucken trophy. You stay away.'

I wasn't going to stay away from Heather. She was kind to me and we weren't doing anything wrong.

She stopped me at the school gate after school one day and said she wanted me to meet her mother.

'You live behind the police station?'

'Yes. In the cottage.'

'Then it's not a good idea that I come over. Your old man, I tell you now, he won't be happy when he spots my head.'

'You've never met him. How do you know that?'

'Cause I do. He's a copper and I'm Abo. I never met a copper who didn't want to get hold of a blackfella and skin him.'

'Don't you say that, Noah.' She was angry. 'He's not like that.'

'And your mother? Bet you never said I'm a blackfella. She'll faint when she sees me.'

Heather smiled, but not like she'd done before. It was the same smile I got from other whitefellas. All superior.

'We want to help you. My mother more than anybody. She has been called.'

'Called? What's that mean?'

'To God. My mother has been called to serve God.'

I wasn't interested in God or being saved, but suspected there could be a decent feed involved and reckoned I had nothing to lose.

We stopped at the picket fence outside the cottage. The old police van was parked out front of the station. I prayed we wouldn't run into her father. I followed her to the front door but stopped when she opened it and walked inside. All of a sudden I felt it was a bad idea to come home with her, but it was too late.

Heather waved at me to follow her inside. 'Come on, silly.'

I walked into the front room. It had carpet on the floor with flowers in the pattern, photographs and paintings on the wall and big couches and seats around the room. I could smell something cooking in the kitchen and was sure it was roast meat. Heather called out to her mother. I heard footsteps in the kitchen.

Heather's mother came to the doorway. She had the same hair as her daughter and also wore it in plaits, which made her look like a schoolgirl herself. She was pretty too, just like Heather.

'Hello!' She ran across the room, threw her arms around me and held me tight. 'Noah, Noah. I have heard so much about you.'

She finally gave up hugging me and took hold of my hand.

'Please, sit down.' She led me to the couch, squeezing my hand all the while. 'It's lovely to have you here.'

I'd never met anyone so happy to see me, including relations I hadn't seen in years. Or my old man whenever he came home from gaol.

'Are you a Christian, Noah?' she asked. 'You do have such a rich Christian name.'

Half my family were the craziest Christians on Earth, speaking in tongues when the spirit took them and taking to the Bible day and night. The other half were outlaws or drunks. That was the half I belonged to.

'Are you?' she asked again, looking anxious all of a sudden.

'Yep, I am,' I lied. 'Grandpa reads me the Bible. Sometimes.'

To be truthful, I'd never seen Teddy do as much as read the side of a soup can, and the only time he mentioned religion was when he screamed *Jesus fucken Christ*, which was a lot of the time.

Mrs Moran insisted I eat dinner with the family. It weren't a good idea. I didn't want to sit across the table from a police sergeant.

'That's nice of you, but I gotta get home before dark.'

'That's fine,' she insisted. 'My husband has to be up at four in the morning. We eat early so that he can sleep and Heather and I have time to ourselves.'

Heather took my arm.

'Please stay, Noah.'

I was sure I could hear the meat sizzling in the oven. My tummy heard it, too, and rumbled.

'Ta, then.'

Mrs Moran looked me up and down, inspecting me close like she'd finally worked out I was a blackfella. She tugged at my shirt hanging out the back of my shorts.

'Do you have hot water at your own house, Noah? And a bathtub.'

'No. We got running water, but it's cold. Teddy, my grandpa, he treats us on a Sunday night. Boils up the copper and we all get a share. My sisters and me wash our hair and all.'

'Well, you must have a bath. There's time before we eat. I'll find you some fresh clothes. We have a clean supply that my husband hands out to drifters.'

I didn't want to be having a bath in a strange house.

'Ta, but a feed is plenty enough.'

'I insist,' she said. 'My husband likes us to be presentable at the dinner table, including guests.'

She put a hand on my shoulder and pulled me towards her.

I looked at Heather for help. She raised her eyebrows, like there was nothing she could do.

The water in the bath had some sort of perfume in it. I lay in the hot water looking up at the ceiling. Although I wasn't a Christian at all, I thought maybe I was in heaven. My new best friend was a white girl with teeth like pearls and her mother seemed to love me like blood. It was weird her making me take a bath, but now that I was in it, I was happy. If something was going to go wrong – if Teddy were here he'd say it's *too good to be fucken true* – it could only be on account of Heather's father, the cop.

I pulled the plug, stood up and climbed out of the bath. I had my back to the door when it opened. It was Mrs Moran. I covered myself with my hands. She took a towel from the rail and held it open.

'Let me dry you, Noah.'

'Nah. I don't reckon. I can do that myself.'

'I'm sure you can,' she said. 'I still dry my Heather. She tells me you have no mother. That must have been such a terrible loss for you. Please, let me.'

I wanted to tell her *no*. To scream it at her. But I'd never screamed at a white person before. Never even said no to one. She walked over to me. I wanted to back away but couldn't move. She wrapped me in the towel, sniffed my neck and stroked the top of my head with her fingertips.

'There you are, darling. A poor, poor boy. You are all such poor, poor boys.'

I looked up at her. She was crying.

PARTY LIGHTS

ETE HAD OFTEN PONDERED THE RANGE OF POSSIBILITIES contributing to his memory loss. Each of them was fanciful, and a long way from the truth. Any reputable doctor or friend, even *the man in the street* knew enough about the limits of the human body to conclude that a decade-long habit of hammering a cocktail of drugs had left holes in Pete's brain. He'd shot, snorted and smoked every substance on the market. As a result, he sometimes had trouble remembering his birthdate and telephone number. On one occasion, after a week of binging underground at an abandoned opal mine, he not only forgot his name but the face he saw in the mirror. On a bad day nobody was more alien to Pete than Pete.

He had no real friends, having been abandoned on account of repeated transgressions. He did have an acquaintance of sorts, a horse-trainer, small-time dealer and fellow drug user, Hester Nixon, who'd injected more ketamine into his body than the gelding he'd trained, Good Luck Grant, to a first place at the midweek meeting in Bourke a year back. The horse had overjuiced on Special K and continued running over the finish line, despite all attempts to pull him up. Good Luck Grant didn't stop until he'd thrown the jockey and run into a nearby swamp. The racetrack steward was no doubt suspicious. The horse was tested, the drug detected and Hester lost his trainer's licence.

'What are you going to do about it?' Pete asked, when Hester told him the story.

'Do? Nothing I can do, except maybe change the name of the pony to No Luck Fucking Grant. That's what I'll do.'

'It might work,' Pete laughed, 'unless they twig that it's the same horse?'

Hester's drug business was no more successful than his horse-racing venture. He downed or gave away more drugs than he sold. While Pete was no admirer of Hester's business sense, he was in awe of the man's constitution. Hester had the ability to load his body with chemicals all night and surface the next day sharp as a tack. Hester also had a remarkable capacity for storing information. In high school he'd earned the nickname *Rain Man* after displaying the unique ability to speed-read the telephone book and subsequently recall every name, address and number. He'd made decent pocket money with the act, fleecing tourists passing briefly through town to visit its single attraction, The Giant Spanner. *Banjanna* – a bullet-riddled sign on the edge of town read – *Home of The Giant Spanner.*

Pete purchased his daily dose from Hester, who bought his own supply of drugs from a rig driver who went by the uninventive name of Convoy. He pulled in regularly at the truck-stop cafe on the edge of town for 'fuel, a feed and a fuck' before beginning the long-haul desert crossing. Convoy's risk was minimal. He had one customer in each town, while those he did business with, dealers such as Hester, had a clientele of misfits, souped-up FIFOs and scab-faced teenagers to deal with.

Pete, not quite the entrepreneur himself, had once attempted to break into the trade, setting up a deal with Convoy without Hester's knowledge. His plan was to introduce drugs to the blackfella outstations and sell direct to the Vietnam veterans scattered across old mining leases in the nearby hills. The vets tended to surface in town once a month to stock up on food, drugs and dynamite, and they bought their gear from Hester. Pete would cut Hester out by taking the product on the road, delivering to the customers' doorsteps.

This entry into venture capitalism quickly fell apart. In a small town like Banjanna there were no secrets. The news quickly got to one of the blackfella head-men, Frederick Moss. Sadly, for Pete, Frederick was a man who knew the law of the street just as well as he did the *lore* of the community he took care of. Frederick came hunting Pete and found him dozing under the old blue gum out front of the weighbridge one Sunday morning. He leaned over Pete, shook him gently by the shoulder and whispered a word in his ear. Before Pete could rouse himself Frederick was laying into him with a lump of wood. Afterwards, bloodied, bruised and unable to breathe on account of several broken ribs, Pete lay on his back, sucking for air and moaning in pain. Frederick, his skin as black as coal, spoke in a deep voice. The words were eerily transmitted across the sky from one end of town to the other. 'Bring ya poison near my young ones,' he cautioned, 'and I will strip ya of skin, smoke ya head and eat ya fucken kidney fat – just for beginnings.'

Pete dropped the idea for his drug business that same morning and decided to stick to what he knew best, getting as stoned as Uluru anytime he got the chance.

Pete was sitting at a table under an umbrella out front of the truck-stop one afternoon studying a glass of water when Hester asked if he would like to invest in a croquet lawn for the town.

'I'm giving you an early option Pete. This could bring big dollars into town. We've got nothing here.'

'Course we do. What about The Spanner?'

'The Spanner can go fuck itself. It's an embarrassment.'

'It's no such thing. Just now, on my way here, I saw a busload of Chinese people. Or Japanese people. They were heading out to see The Spanner. Taking photographs. They love it. You know, pineapples, koalas. All that big stuff.'

'Maybe they do. But it brings fuck-all money to town. They spend five minutes taking photographs on them *selfish* sticks and then they piss off. They don't buy nothing. What the fuck was the Council thinking when they had The Spanner put in on the edge of town? The worst decision we ever made. They should have stuck it smack in the centre. We could've parked an ice-cream van across from it and made a killing.'

'Why do you care, Hes? You've got your own business.'

'I care because I'm thinking of running for Council myself one day. People need to see that I have initiative.'

'And a croquet lawn is your way of showing it? Fuck me.'

'I'd bet the viability of a croquet lawn against The Spanner any day of the week.'

Charlie Jackson, the Councillor responsible for the planning decision at the time The Giant Spanner was being voted on, and also the current mayor, was sitting two tables across from Pete and Hester and heard every word Hester said. Before going into politics, Charlie had been unpopular, building what he spruiked as *the largest factory pig farm east of the state border.* He put small farms out of business overnight. Charlie waved at Pete and Hester and smiled with genuine pleasantness. There was little that offended the man. During the election campaign he'd promised *a major new attraction to revitalise this town.* Posters of his smiling face and auburn toupee had been wallpapered on every street. Within twenty-four hours the posters had been defaced with a crudely painted red penis. One of Jackson's cronies, spotting an offending dick on a poster outside the railway station, ran into Charlie's office screaming, *We gotta take them down!*

Charlie wouldn't hear of it. *Democracy in action*, he called the act of vandalism when talking to the sole reporter of the local newspaper the following morning. Alongside the planned construction of The Giant Spanner, Charlie turned the slogan into his election platform.

The decision was ridiculed and Charlie was endlessly mocked behind his back. He was called an idiot and a dickhead. But what few people understood about Charlie Jackson was that he was a political genius. The offending posters became a key talking point of the campaign. They remained in place and

Charlie made speeches repeating the words *democracy, democracy, democracy*, over and over.

While few in town cared for the concept of democracy, suspiciously labelling it a big city invention, Charlie had somehow managed to reinvent himself as *a man of the people* and was never more popular. He killed the election. The following night he had police block the main street, had the posters torn down and organised a bonfire at the main intersection. Charlie quickly reverted to type, ending his victory speech with an ambit threat: 'If the fuckers responsible for this shit don't think I'll find you, you're wrong. And when I do, the arm you used to paint the offending organ with shall be ripped from its shoulder socket and fed to my pigs.'

What would become Hester's final purchase from Convoy led to his downfall. He and Convoy met in the Ladies toilet at the truck-stop. Hester rattled off a list of goodies he was after, to which Convoy replied *Yeah, got it, got it*, without listening to a word of what was said. Hester handed Convoy a roll of notes and received a green supermarket bag in return. As was their usual method of exchange, Hester waited in the toilet until Convoy had jumped into his rig and driven onto the highway. Hester sat on the toilet, reached into the bag and retrieved a solid pouch of weed. He opened it, stuck his nose inside and drew in the scent. He then plucked a bud and rubbed it between his thumb and fingers. The quality wasn't great and marijuana was well out of fashion in the district but once he repackaged it, he'd be able to sell it on to the young kids and ageing hippies. Hester continued to rummage through the range of lollies in the supermarket bag. He tipped the contents out of the bag and looked down at the sachets and bottles of pills of various colours, none of which were labelled. Most of the drugs looked unfamiliar. Convoy had ripped him off. Hester was able to identify no more than two slim bags of coke and what he guessed were ecstasy, on account of the ! stamped on one side of each tablet. The remaining contents of the showbag were a mystery.

Hester dropped a couple of the tablets and walked to his van at the caravan park – *Little Miami*. Sitting in the van, sniffing one of the bags of coke, Hester mulled over how to best move the unidentifiable drugs. It took two further snorts of coke and another tablet for him to realise a solution. He opened several cupboards until he found a large wooden bowl. He then poured the contents of each pill bottle into the bowl, mixed them together, and beat them with the handle of a screwdriver until he'd ground the pills to a fine powder. He added the remaining bag of coke, kept a sachet of what he believed were the ecstasy tablets for himself, and mixed the concoction together.

It was hard work. By the time he'd finished Hester's shirt was drenched in sweat. He ran his fingers through the pale coloured powder, speckled with ruby-red grains. As he moved the bowl to the kitchen sink he noticed that the red crystals sparkled and came to life. The drug took on a hallucinatory quality without him having sampled it. Hester's heart raced with excitement, convinced that he was onto something big. He quickly calculated that after cutting the powder further, he could produce around a hundred deals. The product would need to be sampled, not for precautionary reasons, but in order to *fashion the narrative*, a few of the many business buzzwords he'd picked up after watching *The New Entrepreneurs* on cable TV. The young presenter of the program, who'd become a millionaire by the time she was twenty-one, apparently selling heated slippers online, was forever reminding viewers about the secret of her success. 'Whenever you have plans to put a new product in the marketplace, it is vital that you also produce a narrative and eye-catching branding to seduce the buyer.'

Hester emptied the contents of the bowl into a plastic bag, sealed it with an elastic band and searched the van for his mobile phone, without success. He left the van and walked the pathway separating two rows of caravans. A boy on a pushbike rode towards him. Hester had seen the kid around the park. He never seemed to be at school and wore a pair of permanently blackened eyes. Each time they were on the verge of fading, fresh swelling and bruising appeared. The boy rode past Hester, turned and pedalled alongside him.

'You got something for me?' he asked.

Hester walked a little quicker. 'Fuck off, runt.'

'Fuck off yourself. You got any drugs?'

'I don't know what you're talking about.'

'You do so. And if you don't give me some I'll call the cops.'

Hester stopped on the roadway and grabbed the handlebars of the bike.

'You go to the police, retard. You know what they'll do? Your family will be put in a cage and paraded around the town, you fucken hillbillies. Piss off.'

Hester yanked the handlebars of the bike, a little too hard, and the boy fell off. He lay on his side and cried. Hester didn't want to attract the attention of the kid's family. They may have been dirt poor but they could fight like bulls. He helped him to his feet.

'I'm sorry, kid. It was an accident.'

He brushed dirt from the boy's T-shirt, reached into his side pocket and pulled out the sachet of ecstasy tablets.

'Hold out your hand,' he said, and poured half a dozen tablets into the boy's palm. 'There you are. Now, don't take them all at once. And maybe stay off the pushbike. On the roads, at least.'

The boy looked down at the tablets in his hand and smiled. 'Ta.' He swallowed one, jumped on his bike, screamed 'Whoop! Whoop!' and rode away. Hester walked to the front gate of the park, stepped into the public telephone box and made a call.

'What?' Pete shouted when he picked up the phone. He sounded like a man who'd been rudely interrupted from a matter of great importance.

'Meet me out by The Spanner,' Hester said.

'Why?' Pete shouted again.

''Cause I have something for you.'

'What?'

'A treat,' Hester giggled. 'A real treat.'

The Giant Spanner, stretching towards the clear afternoon sky, was secured behind a three-metre high fence topped with razor-wire. It was guarded by a CCTV camera, which may or may not have been in working order. The Council had deemed the security a necessary defence of the landmark tool following repeated acts of vandalism, including a graffiti tag identical to the penis that had desecrated the face of the would-be mayor. When Hester arrived, Pete was sitting in the red dirt, resting his back against the wire fence. Hester strode across to him and dropped the bag of powder at Pete's feet, then looked up and glared into the warm ball of sun. The head of The Giant Spanner resembled a prehistoric monster.

'Where's my treat?' Pete shouted. 'You got nothing, you fucking liar.'

Hester bent down, picked up the bag and held it by the handles, slowly swinging it from side to side like the pendulum of a grandfather clock.

'I do have it. And it's a fucken wonder.'

Pete licked his lips and reached for the bag. Hester stepped away from him. 'Not so quick. Let me show you what I've got.'

He took a dirty handkerchief from his pocket, unfolded it and laid it in the dirt. He untied the supermarket bag, reached in with his fingers and tipped a small mound of powder in the middle of the cloth. It glowed and sparkled in the sunlight. Pete's eyes lit up.

'What is it, Hes? It looks … alive.'

'What it will be, very soon, is the newest product on the market.'

'What do they call it?'

'Doesn't have a name. That's how new it is. I'm going to break it down and sell it myself. I have to come up with a product description. Something that will stick. You have any ideas?'

Pete moved closer to the handkerchief.

'Look at the way it's winking at us. Remember the old

Angel Dust? Now that was a drug,' he momentarily reminisced. 'Maybe you could call it Fairy Dust. Something like that. You know, because of the way it's sparkling.'

'Nah. I want something more original than that.'

Hester stared into the glowing powder. He waved his open palm over it and felt a sense of warmth on his fingertips.

'I know. *Party Lights.* What do you think?'

'*Party Lights.* Yeah. I like it. What's it do for ya?'

'You're about to find out. Pinch yourself a decent snort, Pete. It's on the house. Get it right up there in the membranes and we'll see if you go off.'

Pete hesitated. 'Do you think it's safe?'

'I hope not,' Hester grinned. 'We'll see how close you can get to the sun without burning up.'

No sooner had Pete shot a pinch of the powder up his nostril than his eyes lit up. They changed colour from bright yellow, to red, to deep blue. His body shook for several seconds and relaxed. He fixed a dreamy smile on Hester.

'What's it like?' Hester asked. 'Is it good gear, Pete? Is it good?'

'I've found it. I've found it,' Pete babbled.

Hester grabbed Pete by the shoulders and shook him lightly. 'Found what?'

'The world,' he smiled lazily. 'I found the world. The beautiful world.'

Pete looked happier than Hester had ever seen him. His face radiated joy. Hester was so excited he dropped to his knees, scooped a handful of powder out of the bag and buried his face in it, sniffing and snorting like one of the mayor's hungry pigs at a trough of feed. He lurched forward and his face slammed into the red dirt. He could hear Pete calling his name but was unable to move. He rolled onto his side and slowly opened his eyes. He smiled at Pete, who was hovering above him with a demented grin. Pete offered a helping hand. 'Come on, Hes. We're off.'

'Where to?'

'I haven't worked it out, but we have to go.' He pointed along the highway. 'Out there. It's out there. The world.'

Hester had difficulty hearing what Pete was saying on account of the brass band playing in his head. They decided on a second snort each before venturing on their way. Pete took Hester by the hand, like a gentle father guiding an anxious son. Some way down the road Hester looked back over his shoulder and saw a large hole in the ground, where The Giant Spanner should have been wedged into the earth. It was gone. He looked to Pete for an explanation, but Pete was busy, head tilted back, gazing into the sky and admiring the cotton clouds meeting the glow of a setting sun.

The brass band began playing the first bars of the national anthem. Hester shook his head violently from side to side in an attempt to free himself of it.

'I'm no fucken patriot,' he shouted at Pete.

'What?' Pete shouted back.

'Forget it.'

Unable to dislodge the tune Hester had no choice but to begin marching along the highway towards the desert. Pete couldn't hear the music at all, but fell into step with his friend.

Up ahead they could see a yellow front-end loader working alongside a large wooden house. The windows of the house were shattered and the timber boards were splashed with graffiti.

The loader moved backwards and forwards gouging buckets of earth out of the ground. The hole was around ten metres deep and twice as wide.

As they marched closer, Hester noticed the driver of the loader possessed a remarkably rich head of silver hair. The man sat watching as they goose-stepped closer. Hester stopped and stared into the hole. Pete ignored the hole completely. Instead, he thrust an arm in the air, as if trying to grasp the final rays of the setting sun in his hand. The driver killed the loader's engine and jumped down, standing over the hole and admiring his work.

'Hey,' Pete called to him, 'you dug a big hole.'

'I did,' the man nodded, appreciatively.

'Hey,' Hester called out. 'Have you seen a giant spanner come by this way?'

'I did, indeed.' The driver pointed west. 'It was headed that way. Flying low and fast into the sun.'

Pete was having trouble concentrating. He wandered around the edge of the hole to where the driver began rolling himself a cigarette.

The driver offered his hand. 'Jerry.'

Pete shook Jerry's hand. He couldn't remember his own name but was happy to introduce Hester, who trailed behind. Hester also shook Jerry's hand.

'For what purpose have you dug this hole?' Hester asked.

Jerry was not a man to offer a word more than he needed to. 'For filling it in.'

'With what?' Pete asked. 'The dirt you just took out of it?' He giggled.

Hester thought the comment worthy of a laugh and chuckled. Jerry took the question more seriously. 'You would be correct. Eventually most of the dirt will be returned to the hole.' He pointed in the general direction of the old house. 'First off, I'll be pushing this place into the hole and then I'll bury it.'

'You're going to bury a house?' Hester said. 'Why would you do that, Jerry?'

'Most of all because it's cheap and quick,' Jerry answered. 'I get paid to demolish and remove derelict buildings from sites. One time I used to cart these houses away on the back of a truck, find a tip that would take them and pay a large fee. One day I was looking at an old barn I was about to take down, and this idea came to me. What do they call them? Light bulbs or something?'

Hester looked across at Pete and shrugged.

'I think it must be something like that. A light bulb,' Pete offered.

'You boys want to watch me go to work? Show you how efficient the process is?'

Hester wasn't sure if he wanted to see a house buried in the ground, but thought it would be rude not to show interest in Jerry's enthusiasm for his work. 'Yeah, we'd like to see that, Jerry. Wouldn't we Pete?'

Pete had lost interest in Hester, Jerry, the house and the hole in the ground. He returned his attention to the setting sun.

Jerry hopped into the saddle of the front-end loader and drove off, rumbling across the ground, the motor spewing dirty smoke as it disappeared behind the house. Moments later the sound of breaking glass and splintering timber filled the sky. Hester watched in morbid fascination as the house tilted forward, breaking free of its rotting foundations. The sides of the house opened up, leaving the body clinging to the loader. It tumbled over the edge of the hole, rolled onto its roof and crashed into the pit, sending a cloud of red dust into the air. Hester covered his mouth and coughed. The loader mopped up the remains of the house, pushing ends of timber, glass and broken roof tiles into the ditch. Jerry filled the bucket of the loader with dirt and started filling in the hole, repeating the process until the house had disappeared. He then used the empty bucket to level and flatten the earth above the buried house. Within minutes there was little evidence the house had existed at all except for the red-gum footings poking out of the earth, resembling a set of rotting teeth.

Hester looked down at the disturbed patch of ground, mesmerised by what he'd witnessed. Jerry walked across to him. 'I must be on my way, son.'

'Where you heading?' Hester asked.

Jerry looked across the flat horizon. 'For a man in my position, the work never ceases. I'm about to head to another house, another hole in the ground. What's going on with your friend here?' he asked. 'He seems to be out of sorts?'

Pete had been hypnotised by the late afternoon sun. He stood still as a statue, marvelling at the sky and the streaks of colour shooting low on the horizon.

'Don't worry about Pete. He's always been curious.'

Jerry again shook Hester's hand. 'I'll be on my way.'

He jumped into the loader and drove onto the highway. Hester rested on his haunches and watched as the lights of the loader gradually disappeared into the looming darkness.

'You ever see anything like that before?' Hester asked Pete.

Pete scratched his head. 'Not sure. I can't say, Hes.'

'Can't say? I'd never forget it, if I'd seen something like that before, a man burying a whole house.'

'Well, Hes. You don't possess the skill set that I do. I can forget most things when I put my mind to it.'

Pete yawned. He suddenly felt very tired. He lay in the dirt alongside Hester. Within minutes he was asleep. He did not wake until early the next morning. Hester was asleep beside him, face down in the dirt. Pete nudged him in the ribs. Hester groaned and lifted his head. His body was covered in fine red dirt. He sat up and looked around. 'Where are we?' he asked

'On the side of a road, I'm guessing.'

Hester got to his feet and dusted himself down. 'There was something here, wasn't there, Pete?'

'There's always something some place. Which way's town, you reckon?'

Hester pointed east and then west. 'Could be that way. Or maybe that way. I'm heading this way. West. You coming?'

'Not sure yet.'

'Well, I'll see you when you make up your mind.'

Pete watched as Hester walked out along the highway, tracing his own long shadow. He thought about following but had failed to decide by the time Hester had vanished into the distance. He walked across to a circle of ground and dropped to his knees. For reasons he would never be able to comprehend Pete started digging with both hands.

LIAM

IN THE YEAR OF HIS SIXTEENTH BIRTHDAY MY UNCLE LIAM spent time in youth lock-up after a robbery on a newsagency. The shop was run by a Mr Quigley who'd fought in New Guinea during the war. Although he never spoke of his experience, Quigley returned home traumatised and would often wake in the night screaming with rage. His wife died two years after his return and Quigley was left to cope alone. It didn't take long for his life to fall apart. It was common for him to politely greet a visitor to the shop only to abuse the same person minutes later. He once threw a handful of coins at a customer and the police were called. When newspaper proprietors, confectioners and tobacconists would no longer supply the shop with goods, Quigley's business collapsed. The shop remained open nonetheless. Newspapers and magazines, some many months old, their corners nibbled at by mice, sat on the shelves unsold. When unsuspecting customers entered the newsagency and were confronted by the mumbling shopkeeper wearing nothing but a moth-eaten dressing-gown and reeking of urine, they made a quick exit.

Although he appeared to live in poverty, a rumour circulated the neighbourhood that Quigley kept large amounts of cash secreted inside the shop. The story of a hidden stash took on the status of myth and the supposed hundreds of pounds soon grew into thousands, eventually tempting a pair of teenage boys to rob the old man. One of the robbers was Liam, the youngest of my grandmother's four children, a deceptively sweet faced boy with a head of rich auburn hair and large brown eyes. Liam had run wild from a young age. My grandmother did her best to rein him in, but had little control over a boy she admitted herself was *born for trouble*.

Liam broke into the newsagency late one night with his friend, Martin Caton. Well after Quigley had locked up the shop and gone upstairs to bed they jemmied the side door with a pinch bar and began ransacking shelves and cupboards. Unknown to the boys, Quigley was awake, having been stirred by one of his night terrors. He heard the commotion and tore down the stairs screaming a war cry. When Quigley reached the landing, he fell and tumbled into the hallway breaking a shoulder bone and several ribs. Liam went to investigate and saw Mr Quigley on the ground moaning in pain. He and Martin panicked, left Quigley where he lay, and ran from the shop.

The pair were arrested two days later. The evening before, Martin had been out on a date with a girl at the local movie theatre and bragged about what he and Liam had done. She went home that night and told her father, a prison warden, who walked straight to the local police station and repeated the story. When the officers arrived at the newsagency they found Quigley still lying where he'd landed from the fall. He was unconscious, dehydrated, and had soiled himself. The boys were arrested, remanded and appeared before a judge at the Children's Court two months later, where they each received a custodial sentence as a result of, according to the judge, *an act of extreme cowardice committed against a war hero.*

I would visit Liam with my mother on Sundays. She'd take him a chocolate bar and a bottle of soft drink, a comic book and cigarettes. We'd sit on a bench in the sun, my mother preening her younger brother's unruly hair. Liam had that impact on people. As troublesome as he was, most adored him. I was seven years old, about to turn eight, and couldn't comprehend that at the end of our visit Liam couldn't come home, too.

On his release, a year later, Liam asked my mother if he could stay with us. We lived several suburbs away from where the crime had occurred, and the streets where Liam's teenage friends continued to cause occasional havoc. Whether they might be a bad influence on him, or more likely, that Liam would lead them to trouble, my mother agreed but only on the condition he avoid his old friends. My grandmother, who rarely visited Liam in lock-up, was unhappy about the arrangement. She and my mother argued and stopped speaking to each other. My father was also unhappy about Liam coming to stay, complaining to my mother that our house was already overcrowded. Surprisingly, she got her way, firmly telling my father that the decision to support her brother had been finalised and she wouldn't be going back on it.

Our house was dominated by my father; his physical

presence, his sullen moods, his unpredictable explosions, even the sound of his shuffling work boots in the hallway when he arrived home was ominous. Privacy was non-existent and secrets impossible to keep. My parents shared the front room with a ridiculously oversized club lounge, a twenty-one-inch television set, purchased on the *never-never*, and a radiogram 'three-in-one', old enough to play seventy-eight records. I slept in the second room with my older brother, Matthew, and my three sisters, Margaret, Irene and baby Rose. The room was furnished with a pair of double bunks, one on each side of the room and a cot under the single window for Rose, who was a little over a year old when Liam arrived.

He came only with an army duffel bag my mother bought for him from the disposal store. The bag contained a few spare clothes, a breadboard he'd made for my mother in the lock-up workshop and a pile of dog-eared comic books. Mum decided I'd move down to the bottom bunk with Matthew, allowing Liam to enjoy the top bunk to himself. Irene, who was four, slept in the top bunk across the room. Although initially she was a little fearful of Liam, she couldn't take her eyes off him, and as happened with most people, she soon fell for him. Irene would wake early of a morning and climb down from her bunk and then up the ladder, into Liam's bed. I'd wake to the sounds of him whispering Irene a story that he'd made up, or reading to her from one of his comic books.

Liam had been with us for less than a month when my eldest sister, Margaret, came home from school full of anger. A girl had confronted her in the yard, shouting to other students gathered around them that our family was sharing our house with a criminal, a *murderer*, and that the church would never tolerate the situation if the details were known. She told Margaret she should be expelled, immediately. That afternoon Margaret sat on her bed waiting for Liam. When he came home she asked him directly if he had killed a person.

'Of course not. I swear on your mother's life that it's not true.'

'Well, what did you do wrong to be locked away?'

Liam sat on Margaret's bed and told us the story of the newsagency break-in and said he felt terrible for the trouble he'd caused Mr Quigley.

'It will never happen again. Anything like that.'

Margaret stood up and kissed him on the cheek. 'Thank you, cousin. I believe you.'

Liam took no time settling in. His probation officer arranged a job for him at Stones Timber Mill, not more than a ten-minute walk from our house. He enjoyed the mill and never missed a day's work. If he happened to be passing by on a timber delivery, he'd drop off a load of off-cuts for our fire. Liam also changed the mood of the house with his warmth and humour; he was a great storyteller and never told the same story twice, unless one of us insisted on it. He was able to hold our attention from the first to the last word. After he'd left the front room one night, on a visit to the backyard toilet with a lamp for company, my mother said that if Liam applied himself he could become a writer one day. If she'd mentioned that word – writer – in the same sentence as anyone else in the family, it would have sounded ridiculous. With regard to Liam it made perfect sense.

His influence on the family gradually extended to my father. As Liam told a story my father would poke the glowing fire, occasionally adding a block or two of wood. To everyone's surprise he began sharing stories of his own. While he sometimes stumbled with words, I gradually learned more about his past. He told us about the years he spent on the road with his parents. They had worked as labourers in the fruit-picking industry and moved from town to town, which meant my father had little formal education. He also told stories about his army service, a period of his life he'd never spoken of before.

Months after Liam moved in with us I was doing one of my regular chores, helping Margaret with the Saturday morning shopping. It was her job to go into each shop – the grocer, the butcher and the baker – while I waited in the street with the baby pram that doubled as a shopping trolley. I was looking in the window at the grotesque line-up of decapitated pigs' heads that both frightened and fascinated me, when I felt something lick the side of my leg. I looked down and saw a dog. It was a solid animal with a rich brown coat except for the white socks on its paws. I dropped to my knees and gave the dog a pat. It ran around in circles, wildly wagging its tail, jumping up and licking me.

When Margaret came out of the shop she ordered me to leave the dog alone. I did so, reluctantly. The dog followed us, initially at some distance. We turned the corner at the end of the main street and the dog trailed behind. Margaret tried shooing it away, with little luck. She unwrapped the parcel of meat, took out a chop and waved it in front of the dog's face. The dog snapped at the meat as she pulled it away. Margaret ran into the middle of the road and hurled the chop into a vacant allotment. The dog raced into the empty block, sniffing amongst the weeds and rubbish in search of the meat. As we turned into our street I looked over my shoulder. The dog was nowhere to be seen. We thought we'd lost it until Margaret was just about to open our front gate and the dog came running down the the road with the chop hanging from the side of its mouth.

There had been many occasions when we'd asked my father if we could have a pet. This was a time when dogs were given away free and it was not uncommon for a pup to be left tied up outside the milk-bar for anybody who wanted to take it home. My father would argue that he could hardly afford to feed his own children, let alone an animal. His claim wasn't quite true, of course. My father was no drunk. Not at all. But he enjoyed a glass of beer after work and bought the newspaper every morning. I was convinced all we needed to do in order to afford a dog was to persuade him to give up drinking and reading the paper; an unlikely solution that I knew, even at a young age, could never be suggested to him.

While Margaret and my mother unloaded the groceries that morning I made a peanut butter sandwich and quietly snuck out of the house. I was desperate to play with the dog. I ate half the sandwich and offered it the other half. The dog showed no interest, but followed me anyway. We spent the day together on *the flat*, a scrubby patch of land three streets from home. It was dotted with broken swings, a seesaw, maypole and a slide. The flat was where kids played British Bulldog and learned to smoke cigarettes. One of the older boys playing competition marbles that day got down on his hands and knees behind the dog and told me it was a girl dog.

'This dog has no balls,' he explained.

Another kid, Lenny Kelly, who'd had polio and wore callipers, interrupted. 'That doesn't mean it's not a boy. Some boy dogs have no balls either. I've seen my dad cut them off. Stuck our new pup in a gumboot, headfirst so he couldn't move or bite, and snipped his balls off with a razor.'

Other players who'd gathered around to pat the dog looked at Lenny like he was mental and went back to the marbles game.

By late afternoon, when the time had come for me to go home and light the fire, I didn't know what to do with the dog. I couldn't stop her following me home so I snuck her through the side gate, into the backyard. I tried coaxing her inside the back toilet but she was too smart for me and sprinted excitedly around the yard in wide circles, barking loudly enough to bring my mother outside. She pointed and screamed, *A dog!* Liam was close behind her. He smiled, ran over and tickled the dog behind the ears. My mother shook her head and walked back inside, leaving Liam and me to play with the dog until the sun had gone down. The house across the lane from us was empty and when it was time for us to sit down and eat we hid her in the back shed.

Most days my father finished work on the garbage truck before lunchtime. He would come home, have a sleep and then sit up in bed reading through a pile of paperback westerns. In the late afternoon he'd head for the pub and have no more than two glasses of beer before walking home. My mother could set the clock by his regularity. He'd walk back into the house at ten minutes after six o'clock closing.

The next afternoon, I was playing in the yard with the dog, and was enjoying myself so much I forgot about the time. I was about to put her in the shed across the lane when my father called me into the kitchen for tea, *Now!* I panicked, left the dog in our yard and ran inside. The food was already on the table. While Margaret said grace I prayed that the dog would keep quiet, at least until my father fell asleep in front of the fire, which he usually did soon after we'd eaten.

My mother cooked the chops that night. Dishing up, she complained the butcher had pulled up short. 'How many chops did you ask for, Margie?'

'Twelve,' Margaret answered, without missing a beat.

'Well, there's not twelve here. You keep a watch on him next time. Count them out in front of him if you need to.'

Outside, the dog had picked up the scent of the grilled chops. She yelped and scratched at the back door. My father stood up from the table and pulled the door open. The dog jumped at him. 'What the hell is this?'

In any other circumstances my father would have kicked the dog's arse and thrown her into the street but Liam came to the rescue, saving me and the dog both. He quickly invented a story that the dog had followed *him* home and asked if we could keep it. Liam assured my dad that he'd pay for her food from his own wages, and he'd pick up her mess in the yard and give her a hose down and wash once a week.

'She'll be no trouble,' he smiled. 'Look. She's a beauty.'

We all looked to my father for a response. He fell silent and walked back into the house, one of the few times I remember him resigned to defeat.

We enjoyed that summer with Sally Ann, the name Irene gave the dog, in honour of her closest friend in kindergarten. Sally Ann followed me everywhere I went during the day and slept in the kitchen on a stuffed hessian sack of a night. My father left the house early of a morning for work and once he'd gone I'd fetch Sally Ann from the kitchen and put her under the blankets with me, which annoyed Matthew, as the bed was already crowded. Sally Ann also ate breakfast with the family, enjoying a bowl of milky tea and two slices of buttered toast each morning.

Laying in bed one night, jammed between Matthew and the wall, I heard people talking loudly in the front room. Sally Ann let out a growl from the kitchen. Liam had been to the football that day and hadn't come home. I shook Matthew awake.

'Hey, Matt. They're fighting in there.'

He rolled from his stomach onto his back. 'What?'

'Mum and Dad. I think they must be having an argument.'

He sat up in bed and listened. 'You're having one of your nightmares. Get back to sleep.'

I lay as still as I could until I was sure that Matthew had fallen back to sleep and then put my arm around him for comfort.

The next morning, when I got out of bed to go into the kitchen to get Sally Ann, Rose's cot was empty. In the kitchen my grandmother was sitting at the table, my mother across from her, nursing Rose. Sally Ann lay on her bed, looking mournful. I hadn't seen my grandmother in a long time. She looked terrible. Her hair was a salt and pepper colour and stood on end, while her face was caked with a powder that gave her skin a grey appearance. A young man stood against the kitchen sink drinking tea. He wore a grubby pair of overalls and a work jacket. I didn't recognise him but would learn later that he was Liam's older brother, my uncle Jack.

'Give your nan a kiss,' my mother ordered.

I kissed my grandmother on the cheek and was left with the taste of scented powder on my lips. I felt sick. My grandmother didn't say a word to me. She was looking down at the leaves in the bottom of an empty tea cup. I noticed that the rim of the cup was lipstick stained. My mother ordered me back to my room. 'Get your brother and sisters up.'

I was hungry. 'What about breakfast?'

'You can have it when you get back. I want the four of you off to early Mass.'

Matthew, Margaret, Irene and I got ready and left the house. A Bedford truck was parked in the street. I held Irene's hand as we walked to church, as much for my own comfort as hers. There was something terribly wrong at home and I was sure that Margaret knew more than the rest of us about what was going on.

After Mass she demanded we say a prayer at each of the twelve Stations of the Cross. Matthew refused and waited for us on the stone steps out front of the church. When we got home the truck was gone and so was my grandmother. Inside, the house was deadly quiet and my mother was nowhere to be seen. My father was standing in the kitchen awkwardly nursing Rose. He handed her to Margaret.

Around lunchtime my mother returned home with a steaming package of fish and chips. She opened it at the kitchen table. Such food was a rare treat. We ate together in silence, savouring the meal and holding the tension at bay. Afterwards, my mother put Irene in the cot with Rose, handed her a cloth book and asked Irene to read a story to her baby sister, which wasn't easy, seeing as Irene could hardly read herself. She then ordered us older kids to sit at the kitchen table, where she delivered the terrible news. Liam had been killed the night before.

Without a hint of emotion she told us that after the football match he'd met up with a group of boys, some he'd been in lock-up with. They'd gone to a hotel and then to a party. Later in the night Liam got into an argument over a girl and ended up fighting in a laneway. The fight was broken up and Liam walked away. He was shot minutes later, receiving one bullet to the side of the head and another in the back as he lay face down in the street. My mother didn't shed a tear delivering the news, and seemed unable to console the immediate grief of her children.

In the days and weeks following Liam's death my mother hardly spoke. She went for long walks alone, sometimes for hours. My father did the cooking and house cleaning for the first time in his life. Margaret stayed home from school to take care of Rose and kept a watchful eye on the rest of us. While I asked Margaret endless questions, Matthew, who would always take after my mother, remained silent in the days between the murder and the funeral. Irene missed Liam terribly and asked me where he'd gone to and when would he return. Some weeks after the funeral I took her by the hand, and with Sally Ann at our side we walked the cold streets until we arrived at the entrance to the narrow street where Liam had been shot. Sally Ann sniffed the air. I pointed to the roadway. 'Uncle Liam died here. He won't be coming back. Not ever.'

I took it upon myself to pay for Sally Ann's keep from the money I made selling newspapers after school. I didn't mind. I loved the dog as much as anyone in the family, and caring for her kept me as close as I could be to Liam. But Sally Ann changed after Liam's death. She became an angry dog. A debt collector turned up at the front door one afternoon demanding the money we owed on our time-payment television set. He yelled at my mother and she yelled back at him. He made the mistake of putting a foot in the door. Alerted by the ruckus, Sally Ann barrelled past my mother and clamped her jaws around the debt collector's calf. He retreated, leaving a bloody trail on the footpath. A week later he returned and handed my mother a bill for the 'invisible mending' needed to repair the tear in his suit pants. They argued again and Sally Ann bit him a second time.

The following day a policeman turned up at the house riding a black bicycle. He picked up a broom in the yard and chased Sally Ann with it, waving the stick above his head. She circled him, barking savagely. Eventually he backed her into a corner, broke the broom handle across her back and proceeded to give her what my father would have called *a good kicking*.

Poor Sally Ann was stubborn when it came to authority. Only two days later I was coming home from the flat with Sally Ann at my side. It was getting dark, I was late and began running. We turned the corner into our street and crashed into a Salvation Army major, bowling him over. He'd been handing out prayer cards and collecting donations. He got to his feet, brushed the knees of his pants and barked at me to watch where I was going and to *restrain* my dog. Sally Ann whined and skipped nervously from left to right before leaping at him and taking a chunk of flesh out of his arm. Then she turned and bolted for home.

It didn't take long for the police to come back to the house with a piece of paper granting them authority to take Sally Ann away. They came in a van with a locked cage and carried a large net. She put up a good fight, barking, snapping and tearing at the net with her claws but she soon collapsed with exhaustion and was finally captured. I went to the back of the van, where Sally Ann had her snout pressed against the wire cage. She licked my fingertips. A policeman driving the van hit the car horn and warned us to step away. We stood in the middle of the road until the van had turned the corner at the top of the street. That night I asked my mother where Sally Ann had been taken to.

'She won't be coming back,' she said, coldly. 'Sally Ann needs more space to run around. She's off to a farm where she'll be happy.'

I didn't believe her and said so. 'That's not true. The police would not be here with a net if she was going to a farm. And you didn't ask for permission from me. Sally Ann is my dog, and Liam's dog, and you didn't ask.' I burst into tears. 'You're lying to me.'

My mother, who had still shown no emotion over her young brother's violent death, grabbed me by the throat and slapped me around the head with her free hand. 'Don't you call me a liar,' she screamed. She continued hitting me until I broke away and ran into the yard.

That night, when my father asked where the dog was, my mother handed him a piece of paper the policeman had given her. He read it, stood up from the table and walked out of the house into the street. I cleared the table and helped Matthew do the dishes. Irene and Margaret dried up and put the dishes away. No one spoke. With the kitchen clean, I went out into the street to see what was keeping my father busy. He'd dragged a chair from the verandah onto the footpath and was sitting quietly, the offending piece of paper in one hand – a receipt for a dead dog. I sat down on the footpath alongside him. I heard a police siren off in the distance and the sound of a barking dog in the next street. A second dog joined in, followed by others across the neighbourhood, roused to anger.

PAINTED GLASS

EACH FRIDAY MORNING TOM CAUGHT THE TRAIN to Parliament station and walked through the Fitzroy Gardens to the psychologist's office. While the sessions themselves had been confronting, he enjoyed the walk. The air appeared to freshen once he entered the park and walked past the old mountain ash he'd been familiar with from when he was a child. When he reached the model Tudor Village in the hollow at the centre of the park, Tom would stop, lean over the low fence and cast an eye over the miniature replica houses. As a boy Tom had visited the park often and would circle the perimeter of the village, pursued by his sister, Bec, older by two years. They each had their favourite building, Tom preferring the mill house beside the stream and Bec the farmhouse on the outskirts of the village. She assured her brother that one day she would live on a farm just like this one, where she would raise animals of her own. Bec had once dared Tom to raid the village and with a mischievous grin he had climbed the fence. By the time their mother realised what was happening and called to him to get out, Tom was laying in the grass, peering through a window into the bakery. For a few minutes a slightly built boy had been transformed into a giant.

Leaving the park, Tom would cross Punt Road into Richmond and make his way along a narrow street dominated by nineteenth-century terraces, each of them occupied by one medical specialist or another. Tom thought back to the first morning he had knocked at the psychologist's door and was ushered into the waiting room by a young receptionist. The building, although recently renovated, carried the scent of its past, a concoction of coal dust laced with rising damp. He imagined the ghosts of the house hovering in its recesses.

Taking a seat in the waiting room, Tom had opened a newspaper and pretended to read it, while closely watching a woman sitting opposite. She was a nondescript-looking person, younger than him by at least a decade, and soberly dressed in a suit. He wondered if she was making similar observations about him, speculating over the reasons for his visit. The woman stood up and quickly left the room, in a state of distress; a change of mind, Tom wondered? The receptionist looked up from her desk briefly before returning to the computer screen. A few minutes later she called him into the psychologist's room, where Tom was invited to sit in an armchair. He smiled nervously at the man on the other side of the desk. Were the psychologist's life story ever made into a movie, Tom thought, the man would surely play himself. His mop of silver hair was parted down the centre, he wore a pair of round-framed glasses perched on the edge of his beak-like nose, a bow-tie under his shirt collar and a three-piece tweed suit.

That first session had begun with Tom explaining the circumstance that led to his breakdown. He was not the only journalist who'd been let go by the newspaper. Sixty staff members had received redundancy notices on the same day, some of them senior editors. In the compulsory exit interview he'd been reassured that the circumstances of his dismissal were a *macro issue* and that he shouldn't feel personally *inadequate*.

'What did you feel, after the exit interview?' the psychologist asked.

'Nothing really,' Tom shrugged, 'I felt numb. I went home, told my wife, Martha, that I had the flu, and went to bed. For a week.'

'And then a month or so later you drove to the coast. Why?'

'Well,' Tom frowned, seriously considering the question for the first time since the accident. 'I'd been down that way when I was younger, in the first year of high school. A boy in my year, I didn't know him well at the time, he invited me to stay at his parents' beach house. I was surprised.'

'Why?'

'I'm not sure.'

'It's possible that he liked you?' the psychologist asked. 'Did you consider that?'

'Not at the time, no. I kept to myself at school. I do remember wondering why he hadn't asked someone else.'

'Did you enjoy the holiday?'

'Oh, yes. I'd never seen the sea. We slept in a bungalow in the backyard and I lay in a bunk on the first night listening to

the waves. Early the next morning we walked to the beach.'
Tom pressed a thumb and finger to his eyeballs. The psychologist
sat quietly and waited for him to continue. 'I had no idea what
to expect, but was surprised by how beautiful it was.'

'What did you see that morning?'

'Well, the waves were ferocious. They grew louder as we
came over a sand dune above the beach. I was disappointed at
first, when my friend told me it was too dangerous to go into
the ocean. I had no idea what we would do there. Until I saw
the rock pools along the edge of the beach, full of shells and
small fish and straps of seaweed. The sun was warm and we
swam from pool to pool.'

'How did you feel? Do you remember?'

'I felt so happy. And … I know it makes no sense, but even
though I was only twelve years old and I'd never visited the
sea before, I felt like I belonged there. I never forgot it. I often
dreamed about the visit after that weekend …' His voice
trailed off.

'What motivated you to drive to the same beach after all
this time?'

'It sounds strange, but I'm not sure. I hadn't moved further
than from the bed to the couch for a couple of weeks and my
wife was worried about me. Before she left for work that morning
she asked me to drive across the city and collect a parcel for her
at the freight terminal near the docks. A gift from her sister, who
lives in Canada. Martha could have asked the company to deliver
but she was trying to help, to get me moving again.'

Tom took a deep breath and listened to a bird squawking on
a low branch of a tree outside the window.

'I drove out of the freight terminal and got stuck behind a truck. I looked up at a road sign. A left turn would have taken me home, the opposite direction headed to the coast. Without thinking too much about it I turned right and didn't stop driving until I'd parked the car above the rock pools I'd swum in as a kid.'

'And what did you do there?'

'Well, it was very cold. The wind was coming off the ocean and I didn't have a coat. I walked down to the first rock pool. It was the same one I'd swum in as a kid. I was a little shocked, but pleased as well, that it was just as I'd remembered it. After all the years away it seemed so *familiar* to me, although I'd only been to the rock pool that one time. Pretty soon, I forgot about the weather and explored the beach, just as I had thirty years earlier.'

The psychologist brought his hands together. 'How was it?'

'As I had imagined and dreamed. It was beautiful.'

'What else did you do?'

'I left the rock pools, walked further along the beach and came across a sign with information about a breed of bird that nests at the base of the dunes. Arctic Terns. They're quite small and yet they fly here from the northern hemisphere each year. I've read more about them since. They have a memory map within the brain directing them to the same nest each year. They're also very loyal. A pair of birds will mate for life.'

'What do you think caused the car accident?'

Tom shifted nervously in his chair.

'I suddenly felt heavy and could hardly walk. It's hard to explain, but in my body, I felt weighted down. I don't know how long I was there. Before I knew it I was shivering again. I hadn't realised it was raining and my shirt was soaked through. I tried running along the beach, back to the car, but couldn't do it. I could hardly put one foot in front of the other. When I got in the car I panicked. I was desperate to get home. That's the last thing I remember. I woke in the hospital and the nurse told me I had run into the back of a truck on the highway.'

The psychologist rested the palms of his hands on the desk. 'Do you believe it was an accident?'

'I'm sure that it was. I don't know what caused it, but I must have blacked out somehow. Like I said, I was exhausted.'

'Why do you think that your doctor referred you to me?'

Tom looked up at a damp patch in a corner of the ceiling. 'She thinks it will help me to talk with someone. A professional.'

'Do you think she's right?'

The psychologist's directness annoyed Tom. He hadn't expected to be put on the spot. 'I have no idea. You'd know better than me.'

The psychologist knew of Tom's reputation as a journalist and that he was an award-winning writer. 'You were obviously angry about losing your job.'

'I was very angry. And I felt worthless.'

'Do you still feel that way?'

Tom hesitated. He considered an evasive answer but changed his mind. 'Yes, I'm still angry. Maybe more than I was the day it happened.'

'Well, you are entitled to be angry. That's normal, too. We need to find a way to manage these feelings, so they don't harm you. But worthless? You're not, Tom. None of us are.'

★

When Tom's doctor had referred him to the psychologist she'd suggested a twelve-week program. He arrived for his final appointment, greeted by the now familiar scent of the building. The receptionist welcomed him with the same formality as his first visit, and Tom took his seat across from the psychologist with a feeling of ease. Towards the end of the session he was asked how he now felt about himself in relation to work and family.

'Well, when I see my wife leaving for the office of a morning, and I have no work to go to, it doesn't feel good. I wonder what my kids think of me, to be honest.'

'I asked you some weeks ago if you believe that your children love you. Do you?'

'Yes,' Tom answered with a smile that came as a surprise.

'Well, don't worry too much about what they think then. Most children are as resilient as they are thoughtful. And how do you feel about what happened to you, at the newspaper?'

Tom opened his hands and studied them as he considered the question. 'I ran into a journo mate last week, in the supermarket of all places. I was at the end of one of the aisles when I saw her. We had worked on the night desk together, years ago. I thought of hiding from her. How silly is that?'

'Why hide?'

'Because I didn't want to go through the embarrassment of explaining myself, that I'd been sacked. She saw me first, came over and we talked.'

'What did she say?'

'Well,' Tom hesitated. 'She told me I was the best colleague she'd ever worked with. She said I was terrific at my job and always supportive of her.'

The psychologist sat back in his chair and lifted his chin.

'How did it make you feel?'

'I felt good,' Tom said.

The psychologist reminded Tom that they were coming to the end of their final session. As he spoke, Tom began to feel a little anxious.

'We don't have to stop here,' the psychologist added. 'It's up to you, Tom. I'd be happy to go on working with you. What do you think?'

'That would be good,' Tom said, with a sense of relief. 'I'd like that.'

They stood and Tom awkwardly stuck out a hand. The psychologist shook it. Although the gesture was formal it appeared to relax both men. The psychologist loosened his bow-tie and undid the top button of his shirt.

'Apart from your family, what other things do you like to do to relax, Tom? Hobbies?'

'I've always been a reader. And there's the writing of course. Although it's work, it does relax me. I haven't been able to get back to it since I was laid off. I don't have anyone to write for, I suppose.'

The psychologist walked with Tom to the door. 'When I'm stressed, I like to look at art.'

'Art?'

'Yes. I find it contemplative, standing in front of a painting or sculpture. It might help you, with the writing as well as the relaxation, engaging with creativity. Do you spend time at galleries?'

'Not really. I was always too busy.'

'You're not too busy now.'

A thought came to Tom, one he would have kept to himself in the past. 'I used to draw when I was a boy. I kept a sketch book and drew in pencil and charcoal.'

'Did you enjoy it?'

'I did. And then I got a poor school report one term, and my father was so angry he told me I needed to concentrate more. He took the art book and pencils away from me.'

The psychologist smiled faintly at Tom, but did not respond, filing the anecdote away for a future conversation.

Tom walked through the gardens, surprised that the mention of art had reminded him of the drawings of trees and animals he'd once filled his art book with. He'd copied the animals from pictures in a world atlas he'd been given by his parents as a birthday gift. His father had expected he'd learn something from the commentary attached to the pictures, rather than waste his time sketching them.

When Tom reached the other side of the park, instead of heading towards the train station for home, he turned towards the city. He didn't know what he'd discover there, but he didn't stop walking until he was standing outside the National Gallery of Victoria. It was a building he'd walked and driven by many times over the years without bothering to go inside.

He watched a large group of squealing children, some barefoot, playing at the gallery's iconic waterwall entrance. They held flattened palms to the glass and stamped their feet, letting the water splash over their young bodies. One boy went as far as to lean forward and press the top of his head against the glass wall, showering himself with water. Tom watched as a man in shorts and a singlet, most likely the boy's father, moved forward. He was about to scold the boy but when the boy turned, the father saw his beaming face and smiled. To the mildly disapproving look of a gallery staff member the father placed his own head to the wall and drenched himself alongside his son.

Tom entered the gallery foyer and looked up to see a giant ball wrapped in silver foil floating above his head. He turned and looked back at the crowd outside, their bodies distorted by the effect of water running over the glass. With no clear sense of where to begin, Tom rode the escalator to the first floor. He spotted a tour group ahead and joined the back of the line. The guide led them through a room filled with Chinese vases and sculptures, then into an exhibition of period furniture. The guide spoke in the hushed tones of a documentary narrator and Tom could hear little of what was said. He decided to trail off on his own, wandering from room to room until he eventually found himself standing in front of a painting by Vincent van Gogh. Tom looked around. He was alone. He stepped forward to examine the painting more closely and was surprised to see that the brush strokes were clearly visible. He also noticed what looked like a speck of dirt painted into the corner of the canvas and wondered if the artist had purposely left a blemish in the night sky. He had no doubt that he was looking at a genuine artwork, but it did little to move him; a fault of his own and not the artist, he was certain.

Tom made his way back downstairs and ordered a cup of black tea at the ground-floor cafe. He could hear laughter nearby, breaking the solemnity of the gallery. He left his drink and walked in the direction of the ruckus, into the Great Hall, a cavernous space famous for its stained-glass ceiling. The room was filled with children, some jumping on foam sofas, others rolling across the carpeted floor, crashing into parents and grandparents resting their heads on cushions, looking up in childlike wonder. The sounds of the children reverberated from the walls. Tom took a seat at one end of the hall, leaned forward and picked up a brochure from the floor. It explained that the artwork above his head was one of the world's largest stained-glass ceilings, fifteen metres wide and over fifty metres in length.

His reading was distracted by a young child, barely old enough to walk, tight-roping across the room at an increasingly frenetic pace before slamming into a foam chair and falling to the ground. The girl looked up at Tom and frowned. For a moment it appeared she was about to cry. She didn't. The reflection of the soft reds and greens of the stained glass had painted her bare arms. The girl raised her hands and looked with delight at her new skin, as did Tom. He gasped with unexpected pleasure. The girl got to her feet, turned and headed back to her family. Tom looked around the hall before gently easing himself to the floor. He rested a pillow behind his head and looked up at the ceiling. It appeared to be moving, creating a hypnotising effect.

★

When he woke the Great Hall was empty except for a young gallery attendant standing in a doorway at the other end of the room. She checked her watch and looked across the room at Tom. He got slowly to his feet and walked towards her, craning his neck to get a final look at the ceiling. 'I'm sorry,' he said. 'I must have dozed off.'

'It's okay. Plenty of people do. That's why I like working in this room. It's peaceful. Don't you think?'

'Yes, I do. It really is beautiful.'

'The artist who did this, Leonard French, he died recently.'

'Oh, I'm sorry to hear that,' Tom answered, taken aback by the unexpected but genuine sense of sadness he felt.

The attendant looked up. 'Do you know how many pieces of glass comprise the work?'

'Oh, I guess there must be hundreds.'

'Not even close,' the attendant smiled. 'It took Mr French ten thousand pieces of glass to complete the work, using fifty different colours.' She pointed towards a panel directly above her head. 'I don't know if you can see it, but that large triangle of blue-green next to the deep yellow square, that piece of turquoise glass, it's my favourite. It reminds me of the sea.'

Tom followed her gaze up to the triangle, and yes, once prodded to consider it, he could see the patch of sea, a sea he had once enjoyed, floating in the kaleidoscope sky. It was truly magical. And it was art.

'How is it that you know so much about the ceiling?' Tom asked.

'Everyone who comes in here loves it, and they always have questions. I want to be able to help.'

'Are you an artist?'

'No.' She shook her head. 'I'm here to guide people. It's enough for me. Are you an artist?'

'No. I came here to look around. I'm … I'm a writer.'

'A writer. Wow!' She again looked up. 'I'm sure there's plenty in here for you to write about.'

Tom also looked at the colourful ceiling. 'Yes. I think there might be.'

Tom was the last visitor to leave. Outside, the afternoon sun lit up the gallery entrance. A new group of children were entertaining themselves at the waterwall, and people were sitting along the edge of the moat, eating ice creams and taking photographs. Tom noticed a young couple holding hands and kissing. A pair of teenage boys waded through the moat, occasionally duck-diving for coins that had been tossed into the water by passers-by for the price of a wish. Tom stood and watched. A woman seated nearby had removed her shoes, hitched her dress up around her knees and was soaking her feet in the water. She turned to Tom.

'I don't think it could be a good thing, stealing somebody else's wish.'

He didn't know what to say. Although the woman looked a little odd she had a pleasant face.

'They mean no harm, of course,' she went on. 'The innocence of youth. There's so much you don't know when you're a kid. It's what saves you. Growing up is the killer.'

Tom gave her a nod and left the gallery. He made his way

towards the train station, pausing on the bridge. The tea-stained water of the wide river beneath him drifted slowly towards the open sea. He stopped, looked down and contemplated the task of putting words together.

SISSY

SISSY HAD NEVER BEEN ON A HOLIDAY and didn't know anyone at Sacred Heart School who'd travelled much further than the local swimming pool. At best they'd enjoyed a tram ride to the picture theatre in the city, maybe once or twice a year. A girl in the same year at school, Ruby Allison, who lived behind the dry-cleaners with her mother and two older brothers, came back to school after the holidays and told a story about how she'd been to the ocean that summer. Ruby sat in the schoolyard at lunchtime, a circle of girls around her, and talked animatedly about the giant waves and the seals basking on the rocks above the beach. No one else in the group had seen the beach and they had no reason to question Ruby's story. Except that she'd been seen most days helping her mother behind the counter in the oppressive heat of the dry-cleaning shop. If the story was untrue, and Ruby hadn't been near the sea, she'd displayed a vivid imagination, which was hardly surprising. If the girls from the school excelled at anything, it was storytelling. As Sister Josephine often remarked, *Those who have little or nothing have the greatest capacity for invention.*

Each afternoon, following the final bell, Sissy would walk to the House of Welcome on the main street, operated by the Daughters of Charity. She'd join a line at the front gate, queuing to collect a tin loaf of white bread, or fruit bread if she was early enough, and an occasional treat of biscuits, before heading home. She also attended *Girls Club* at the House on Saturday mornings. The sole reason Sissy's mother allowed her to join the club was because the morning ended with a mug of chocolate milk and a buttered roll, followed by a hot bath for every girl. Sissy didn't look forward to bath time. The girls were required to line up in alphabetical order and the bath water was changed only after the Ks – Sheila Kane and Doreen Kelly – had bathed, usually together for the sake of economy. Sissy was sure that more than one girl on the line ahead of her took a pee in the water, out of either spite or necessity. She'd spend all of thirty seconds in the bath, and never put her head under the water let alone wash her hair, which she preferred to do under the cold water tap over the gully trap in the backyard at home, no matter how bitter the weather.

One Saturday morning, as Sissy was about to leave the House, Sister Mary took her aside and asked to speak with her. Although she couldn't think of anything she'd done wrong, Sissy worried that she was in trouble. She asked her closest friend, Betty Reynolds, to wait for her out front and went and stood outside Sister Mary's office door. The nun occasionally looked at Sissy over the top of her steel-rimmed glasses as she wrote in an exercise book. When she had finished, Sister Mary closed the book, picked up an envelope, opened it and read over the details of a typed letter.

'Come in, Sissy,' she said.

Sissy stood in front of Sister Mary and looked down at the navy-coloured habit covering the nun's head. She wondered, as she often did, whether it was true that Sister Mary, along with the other nuns, had a shaved head. She quickly looked away in an attempt to purge herself of the thought. Sister Mary stood up.

'Let me ask you a question, Sissy. How would you like to go on a holiday?'

The thought of a holiday was so foreign to Sissy she couldn't make sense of what the sister had asked her. 'A holiday?'

'Yes. Exactly. Each year the Diocese is contacted by our more fortunate Catholic families. Very generous families offering summer accommodation for those less fortunate living in the inner city. This year, for the first time, our parish has been chosen to nominate several children who we consider suitable. I have nominated you, Sissy.'

The sister caressed the piece of paper she had been reading from. 'This letter is from a family who write that they are interested in taking a girl for the coming holidays. They have a daughter of their own who is about to turn twelve, your own age, as well as a younger son. I have spoken to your class teacher, Sister Anne, and she tells me that you have been a diligent and well-behaved student this year, with excellent examination results. I see this as your reward, Sissy,' Sister Mary smiled. 'What do you think of the idea?'

Sissy wasn't sure what to think. She was reminded of Ruby Allison's story from earlier in the year. Perhaps she could return to the school in the new year with her own story of the ocean? A true story.

'Are you interested?' Sister Mary asked, when Sissy didn't reply.

'Yes …' Sissy hesitated. 'I'll have to talk to my mother about this, Sister. She's never had me away.'

'Of course you would. And I will speak with her also. Your mother has always been a grateful woman. I'm sure she'll be happy for you.'

The sister carefully folded the sheet of paper and returned it to the envelope.

'I want you to take this letter home to your mother. Is she able to read?' Sister frowned.

'Yes. She reads well.'

'Very well then. The details are contained in the letter. You must inform your mother that she will need to make her decision by the end of the week, as there are many girls in the school who would welcome such an opportunity.'

'Yes, Sister.'

Sister Mary took hold of Sissy's hand, a rare display of affection.

'This could be of great benefit to you, Sissy. Many of your people have never enjoyed such generosity.'

Your people? Sissy had no idea which people Sister Mary was referring to.

Sissy walked out into the street and found Betty doing handstands against the front wall of the House of Welcome, exposing her underwear.

'Betty, don't do that!' Sissy shouted. 'You'll get in trouble.'

'I don't care,' Betty said. 'I get in trouble anyway, for doing nothing at all.'

On the walk home Sissy showed Betty the letter and repeated what Sister Mary had said to her. If she expected Betty to be excited for her, Sissy was mistaken.

'I know why Sister Mary chose you,' Betty said, picking a stone up from the gutter and wrapping her fist around it.

'Why's that?' Sissy asked, so pleased with herself she began skipping along the street.

'It's because you have whiter skin than me. And your hair is nicer. Mine's like steel wool and yours is straw. You're exactly what them rich white people want, Sissy.'

Sissy stopped skipping, her cheeks flushed with anger. She grabbed Betty by the arm, stopping her from walking on.

'That's not true, and you know it. The reason I've been picked is because I did the best in class this year. Sister Mary said so. You remember the statue of Jesus Christ I won for getting the top mark for Catechism. The holiday has got nothing to do with my skin.'

'Makes no difference,' Betty smirked. 'It's why you get the best marks, too. White skin equals teacher's pet. That's the way it is. Always has been, and you know it.'

Sissy stamped the heel of her shoe against the bitumen.

'You can't believe that, Betty. I've never heard you talk like this before. You must be jealous.'

'I'm not jealous. I'm ...'

Betty aimed her stone at the street pole on the next corner. She pitched it. The stone skimmed through the air and slammed into the pole. She looked pleased with herself.

'Gee, I'd make a good hunter.'

'Not around here, unless you were after a stray cat, or a rat.'

Betty stopped at the corner and sat on the horse trough that hadn't been drunk from for decades. She had a deep frown on her face.

'What's wrong?' Sissy asked.

'I'm scared for you.'

Sissy sat next to her. 'Scared of what?'

'That maybe you won't come back.'

'Don't be silly. Of course I'll be coming back. It's only a holiday. For two weeks.'

'It doesn't matter what it is. One of my cousins, Valda, the Welfare told her mum, my auntie, the same story, that she was going on a holiday. Valda was excited, just like you are now. You know what happened to Valda? She disappeared.'

'I don't believe it. You're making this up, Betty, because you don't want me to go.'

'So what if I don't?' Betty shrugged. 'Even more than that I don't want you to disappear.'

Sissy stood up and tried skipping away, but couldn't recover her rhythm. She stopped, spread her legs apart, leaned forward and touched her forehead on the footpath, an exercise she'd learned in gymnastics class at school. No other girl had conquered the flexibility exercise. She looked through her legs at her upside-down friend.

'The story is not true and I won't be disappearing.'

'Please yourself,' Betty said. 'Don't blame me when they powder your face even whiter than it is and force you to church every day of the week.'

Three weeks later Sissy was seated on a wooden chair on her front verandah wearing her best dress, a daffodil print, and a matching yellow ribbon in her ponytail. A small suitcase sat at her feet. It contained another three dresses, a blue cardigan, a toilet bag and new socks and underwear. Sissy usually wore her mother's hand-me-down underpants, several sizes too big. She was forever hitching them up as she ran around the schoolyard at lunchtime playing netball. As most other girls battled with the same predicament, the situation caused little embarrassment, except on the odd occasion when a pair of underpants fell around a girl's ankles. Sissy had also made a visit to the Book Depot on Christmas Eve, where she swapped two paperback novels for four more plus the cost of a shilling. The books were also in the suitcase. She was a voracious reader and never left home without a novel in her schoolbag.

Sissy was admiring her dress when she heard the rusting hinges of a gate shriek further along the street. She looked up and saw Betty crossing the road. Betty stopped at the front gate, rested her chin on the edge of a splintered picket and looked down at the case.

'So, you're leaving for your holiday?'

'Yeah. The lady I'm staying with is coming soon to collect me. In her own car.'

Betty leaned a little too heavily on the gate and hung on as it swung open.

'Your dress is so pretty, Sissy. I bet you must be happy that you're going away?'

In the weeks since Sissy had been offered the holiday by Sister Mary her enthusiasm for the holiday had gradually faded. She was no longer sure how she felt.

'I am happy. I was so excited last night,' she fibbed. 'I couldn't sleep properly with the nervous stomach ache I had.'

'So, you're really going then?'

'Of course I am.'

Betty hung her head over the gate and tucked her chin into her chest. Sissy heard her friend sob.

'You okay, Bet? What is it?'

Betty wouldn't answer. Sissy stood up, walked over to her friend and lifted Betty's chin. 'What's wrong with you, bub?'

Betty burst into tears. 'I'm sorry what I said about your skin and being teacher's pet. That was mean of me.'

Although what Betty had said had hurt Sissy's feelings, she'd been quick to let go of the pain. Her friendship with Betty meant the world to her.

'I don't care about any of that stuff. It doesn't matter to me. Honest.'

Betty jumped from the gate, lunged at Sissy and threw her arms around her.

'I'm going to be lonely without you for the rest of the holidays. Promise me that you'll come back.'

'Of course I'll be back. I cross my heart. Two weeks is fourteen days. I'll be home in no time.'

Betty wiped her face, said goodbye in a rush and ran off down the street. Sissy was about to take her seat when Betty popped up again at the open gate. She smiled, *all goofy-like*, Sissy thought. Betty walked over to her, leaned forward and shocked Sissy by kissing her on the lips.

'I love you, bub,' she said, before turning and running off a second time.

A few minutes later Sissy's mother, Miriam, came out of the house.

'Who was that just here talking to you?'

'Betty. She came to say goodbye.'

'She did? It's not like you're going on a world cruise or something. That kid's thick in the head. Like the rest of her mob.'

Sissy was quick to defend her friend. 'No, she's not, Mum. There's nothing wrong with Betty.'

'If that's the case, I'm raising a genius.'

Miriam lit a cigarette and sat on the verandah step, waiting for the stranger's car to arrive. When Sissy had presented her mother with the letter of invitation from the church Miriam had not been as excited about the news as her daughter had expected she would be. Nor did she try hiding her concerns about Sissy going off with a person neither of them had set eyes on.

'We don't know who these people are, Sissy. Or anything about them. Who are they?'

'Sister Mary knows them. She told me that the people who offer holidays are all good families.'

'But does she know them personally? What's written on a piece of paper doesn't mean a thing. One word is all you need to tell a lie.'

'Well, Sister Mary said she is going to come around and talk to you herself. They've had children for holidays before. If they were not good people then Sister Mary would know about it. There's nothing she doesn't know, Betty says.'

'Betty doesn't know a whole lot herself. If I ever come to rely on that kid for the safety of my own daughter I'll throw the towel in and let the Welfare take you off my hands.'

Miriam was even more nervous after reading the letter. She twirled a length of Sissy's fringe around her finger and tucked it behind her daughter's ear.

'So you want to go off with this family?'

'Not if you don't want me to. I can stay here as well.'

Miriam had seen the excitement in Sissy's eyes and didn't want to disappoint her.

'You go, little Sis, and have a wonderful time.'

Tucked into the pocket of Sissy's floral dress was a telephone number and a sixpence coin that Miriam insisted her daughter take with her. Sissy was not to spend the money, under any circumstances, she had been told several times. Miriam explained that the coin was only to be used for an emergency. The telephone number was for Mrs Pellegrino, the Italian woman who ran the corner shop, who was happy to take messages for locals.

'I won't need the money,' Sissy said. 'I bet the family will have their own telephone. Sister Mary said that they are *well off*.'

A car turned into the street, a rare occurrence in the neighbourhood. A couple of boys who'd been playing with a rusting three-wheeler bike chased the car as it slowly moved along the road. Miriam dropped her cigarette and ground it under the heel of her shoe. The car stopped in front of their house, a powder blue sedan that shined like new. It was a small car, Sissy noticed, a two-door without a back seat. She didn't know anyone who owned a car and Sissy had never ridden in one. She raised herself slightly out of her chair to catch a glimpse of the driver. The passenger side window was so clean and shining all she could see was her mother's apprehensive olive-skinned face reflected back to her.

The car door opened and a woman got out. Although it was a hot morning she wore a mauve-coloured woollen suit and a straw hat with matching mauve flowers sewn into the brim, shading her pale skin. She was *so* white Miriam was certain the lady was ill. The woman walked around to the front of the car but remained on the road. Miriam stepped onto the footpath and half curtsied before realising the stupidity of her action.

'I'm Miriam Hall, Sissy's mother.' She turned to the verandah. 'Sissy,' she called. Sissy refused to move from the chair. 'Come and say hello to Mrs …'

The woman stepped forward and held out her hand. Miriam looked down at a set of manicured and polished fingernails.

'I am Mrs Coleman.' The woman spoke in a tone simultaneously husky and delicate, in a voice that appeared it might shatter at any moment. 'And this must be your daughter.'

Sissy stared at the sickly looking woman standing in front of the car.

'Come here and say hello,' Miriam ordered her daughter.

Sissy stood up. 'Hello,' she coughed.

The kids on the trike circled the car several times before

Miriam ordered them to get back to their own place. She did her best to be polite to the visitor, all the while resenting the self-conscious deference she displayed towards a person she did not know or care for. Sissy felt the shame of being both embarrassed of, and for, her mother.

After assuring Miriam that Sissy *will be taken wonderful care of*, Mrs Coleman opened the small boot at the rear of her car and stood back as Miriam loaded Sissy's case into it. Sissy could not take her eyes off the woman's face. Her skin was so opaque that lines of thin veins could be seen running down her cheekbones.

When it was time to say goodbye Miriam did so with as little display of emotion as was necessary. She nudged Sissy towards the open passenger door.

'Go on, bub. You be off.'

Sissy only relented and got into the car when Miriam stepped away from her daughter and retreated to the verandah.

'Go,' she said, with the wave of a hand. 'Off you go.'

It was only after she had buckled herself into the passenger seat and was driving away, seated next to the cold-looking woman in the funny hat, that Sissy grasped the reality of what she'd wished for so desperately weeks earlier. She turned her head and looked back at her mother, standing on the verandah with a hand to her mouth.

The car turned the corner, out of the street, and stopped at a red light at the next intersection. The street corner was crowded with people, all of whom would never take a holiday to the coast, the mountains, or anywhere else. Some would never leave the suburb. Mrs Coleman leaned forward and peered out through the spotlessly clean front windscreen. Sissy watched her face. The woman appeared to be in shock. She pushed the button down on the driver's side door, then turned to Sissy and ordered her to do the same.

'Lock your door, dear,' she said, her voice rising slightly.

Sissy turned to lock her own door and spotted Betty standing on the street corner, staring at her.

'Lock the door,' Mrs Coleman repeated, her voice crackling like a poorly tuned radio station.

As the light turned green Betty smiled at Sissy and nodded her head up and down. The car lurched forward, broke suddenly and stalled. An elderly man had walked in front of the car. Sissy grabbed the door handle and jumped from the car before Mrs Coleman realised what was happening. She bolted past Betty, screaming, 'Come on, you slow coach. Run!'

Betty had always been the faster runner of the two girls. She drew alongside her friend within a block. 'Where we racing to, bub?'

'I don't know,' Sissy gasped, 'I'm just running.'

'Come with me then, and hide.'

Betty took off and Sissy followed. They didn't stop until they reached the local football ground several streets away. Sissy followed Betty behind the old grandstand at the far end of the oval. They crawled on their hands and knees into the darkness beneath the stand and gathered their breath.

'You're going to be in such big trouble,' Betty said. 'Sister Mary will kill you.'

'She sure will. I don't care.'

'And your mum, she'll probably kill you, too. After Sister Mary's finished with you.'

'No, she won't. My mum didn't want me to go on the holiday in the first place.'

'You sure of that? I thought you said she was happy for you to go?'

'She was only trying to be happy. It wasn't working. You know them worry lines she has above her eyes? Well, they were bulging out of her head today. I've never seen them worse. It was a sign.'

Betty grinned, as wide as a girl could.

'Well, even if Sister does kill you, I'll still be happy that you never went away in that car.'

'The car! Oh bugger,' Sissy said. 'My case is in the boot. I'll never get it back now.'

'Did it have anything good in it?'

'Yeah. My dresses and some books. And, hey! New undies and socks. I mean brand new underpants from *The Junior Shop.*'

'New undies!' Betty squealed. 'I wish I had a pair of new undies, instead of wearing my mum's bloomers.'

'Me too,' Sissy laughed. 'But it's too late now. And it doesn't matter.'

'Why's that?' Betty asked.

'Because I'm home, Betty. I'm home with you.'

'I knew you wouldn't go off with a strange lady.'

'No, you didn't.'

'I did so.'

Sissy climbed down, sat in the dirt and looked up at her friend.

'Tell me the truth. Did your cousin, Valda, really disappear when she went on a holiday?'

'Of course, she did.' Betty jumped and landed next to Sissy.

'She disappeared for a week. She ran away and showed up back on my auntie's doorstep.'

'You never told me that part of the story.'

'No I didn't. It was better to concentrate on the best part. That's how stories work.'

FRANK SLIM

VIOLA FELL FOR THE BOY AT FIRST SIGHT, leaving her no choice but to care for him. Her brothel was orderly and maintained rules, and near the top of the list was that her girls couldn't bring their kids into work. It was a decision governed by common sense. Viola had a solid relationship with the local police, one that didn't come cheap. Every copper at the station, from senior detectives to young recruits on the beat, put a hand out to look the other way. Social Welfare was a different story entirely. They couldn't be accommodated with either sex or money. Any evidence that a minor had frequented a brothel and the business would be threatened with closure. So, when Else Booth turned up at work one afternoon with a ten-year-old boy, Viola was ready to read the riot act to her. Else raised a hand in her defence.

'I know the rules, Vee, no kids. I only need to leave him for a couple of hours. There's an emergency I have to deal with tonight.'

'Like what emergency?' Viola asked, suspiciously. 'You're paid well here, Else. You have no excuse for working off the books.'

'It's nothing like that. This morning I got a call from one of my mum's neighbours. She's had a fall and has been taken to hospital. They're keeping her in and I need to visit. Take in some soaps and a nightie for her.'

The boy stood in the doorway, looking down at the wooden floor, listening to every word. He was slightly built, delicate even, and wore his dark hair long. The child could easily be mistaken for a girl.

'How bad is she, your mother?' Viola asked.

'I won't know until I see her.'

The house cat, Easy, wandered into the kitchen, looked up at the boy and nestled at his feet. He kneeled and petted the cat.

'Okay, you go then,' Viola said, 'but be back here by five o'clock to pick him up. I can't have him around when the show kicks off.'

Else said, 'Thanks, Vee,' and kissed Viola on the cheek. She walked over to the boy and asked him to stand up. She lifted his chin and whispered, 'I'll see you soon,' before hugging him and leaving the house by the back gate. Soon after, Viola heard a car exit the laneway in a hurry. A woman driven by experience and intuition, Viola knew in that moment that Else would not be back at five o'clock, or anytime soon.

Viola turned to the boy. 'What do they call you, love?'

He raised his head and said, 'Gabriel', in a whisper.

Viola had not seen a more beautiful child. His cheeks were flushed rouge, he had long eyelashes and his deep brown eyes, seeped with sadness, reinforced a sense of innocence. Viola, a hard woman at the best of times, could not avoid touching him. She ran the back of her hand across his cheek and through his hair. 'You must be hungry. Sit down and I'll make you a sandwich and a cup of tea.'

As the girls shuffled in for the evening shift, they were equally taken with the boy. More than one of them referred to him as a *little angel*, without knowing his name. That night he slept in Viola's room, on the chaise longue in the bay window, beneath an expensive Persian blanket that one of her regular customers had given her as a gift. Although she hadn't worked the floor for years, many of Viola's favourites continued to visit. She would pour them a drink, sit and reminisce about *the old days* before sending the men upstairs with one of her girls, thirty years younger than the client, at a minimum.

Gabriel sat and quietly ate breakfast at the table the following morning. The boy didn't ask about his mother, not that day, the day after, or in the weeks that followed. Else's name was rarely mentioned and no explanation for her disappearance was asked for or offered. Viola suspected that one of Else's regulars had fallen for her and promised her something more than working nights in a brothel. Other girls had been swept off their feet in the same manner but such arrangements rarely included taking on responsibility for a child and were generally doomed to failure. Sometimes the proposed elopement was a ruse; the new boyfriend secretly intent on putting his lover to work. A pimp took a bigger slice of earnings than a brothel madame, was about as reliable as a cheap watch and easily roused to use his fists.

Sitting across from the boy that morning, Viola realised she was about to break her own cardinal rule. Later that day she sent the house manager, Johnny Circio, out to buy a single bed and set it up in her room. Viola also handed Johnny a roll of notes. He was to take Gabriel into a department store in the city and get him a new wardrobe and a haircut.

'Why this kid?' Johnny asked, after returning to the house with shopping bags full of new clothes, shoes and underwear for the boy. 'I thought you don't like kids?'

'Maybe I feel sorry for him?' she answered casually, attempting to hide an immediate and deep affection for the boy she could hardly explain to herself.

Johnny laughed. 'Come on, Viola. You've never felt sorry for anyone in your life.'

She didn't like being challenged and put him in his place. 'Mind your business, Johnny. I pay you to keep this house in order, not interrogate me. If you feel a need to behave like a copper, go get yourself a sheriff's badge and a bad haircut.'

'Take it easy, Vee. I'm only asking. He seems like a sweet kid.'

Viola stood at the bay window, parted the velvet curtain and looked out to the street.

'He is sweet. I don't know how, growing up around Else. I've had more than fifty girls come through here and none of them have been as wild as her. He looks as innocent as a doe, and I want it to stay that way. Be sure he doesn't go upstairs and keep him away from the side door, so he's not running into customers. Or police coming by for the collect.'

'So, I'm supposed to be a babysitter now?'

'You're what I pay you to be. I don't want the dirt of this place rubbing off on him. By the way, I need you to get him into school. You can put him down the road with the nuns. Use your home address.'

'The nuns? What if they find out he's living here with you? They'll kick him out.'

'No they won't. They'd only work harder on saving him. If we send him to one of the state schools and they find out he's here, the head teacher will be on the phone to Welfare in a blink and he'll be put straight in a Home. One quality I've always admired in the Micks; they never give up on a wayward soul. They'd have persevered with Hitler.'

Viola enjoyed having the house to herself after breakfast time. The girls were gone by seven in the morning and the house was cleaned and empty by nine. She'd make herself a pot of tea and send Johnny off with the laundry and a shopping list, leaving her to sip her tea and read the newspaper. Johnny had enrolled Gabriel at the local Catholic school and while the boy was not overly familiar with learning, he seemed to enjoy the new experience of having a regular routine.

One morning, soon after Viola had kissed Gabriel on the cheek and sent him off to school, she noticed his lunchbox on the kitchen table. A few minutes later she heard a noise at the side door and assumed he was returning home to fetch it. She got up from the table, walked into the hallway and looked across at the brass knob on the door. She watched as it was turned one way and then the other, followed by a loud knock.

Viola opened the door. 'Gabriel, what are you …'

She looked into the dark eyes of Des Mahoney. He was a small-time criminal with a reputation for thieving from street prostitutes and backyard bookies, people with no place to turn when they'd been robbed. Mahoney hadn't done any prison time, a clear indication that the man was also a police informant; any decent criminal avoided him. There were also rumours he had an attraction to younger girls. The stories alone were enough for Viola to despise him.

'What do you want at my door?' Viola asked, displaying as much hostility as she could muster. 'We're shut.'

Mahoney closed one eye and fixed on her with the other.

'I was looking for one of your girls, Else Booth. She owes me money.'

'Too bad. She hasn't been here for weeks.'

'When's she due back?'

Viola noticed that Des had stuck a foot in the doorway. She rested an open hand on the back of the door, in case she needed to slam it in his face. 'She won't be back. Else has moved on.'

He shook his head, feigning disgust. 'That's no good to me. I got hold of some perfumes for her. French gear. She hasn't paid me for 'em.'

As far as Viola was concerned the perfume story stunk.

'You've waited some time to collect, Des. Like I said, she's not coming back. You'll have to track her down yourself.' She tried to close the door, jamming his boot.

'I need the money,' he snarled.

'I don't have time for this. I'm busy.' She pushed her shoulder against the door, shutting it in his face.

Viola went into her bedroom and opened the curtains on the sunny morning, feeling a little anxious about Des Mahoney. It wasn't uncommon for a customer to knock at the brothel door after hours, and sending them on their way caused no drama. But Mahoney had unnerved her in a way Viola was not used to. She decided to calm herself by running a bath and was about to take off her dressing gown when she heard a creaking floorboard in the hallway.

Des Mahoney pushed the door open. He was holding a knife in his hand and smiling at Viola, a mouthful of rotting teeth on display. Viola studied the knife. The blade was short, maybe only three inches long, but well sharpened, by the look of it. Without a weapon in his hand she wouldn't have hesitated to take Mahoney on. Viola had battled many men over the years, and had the scars to show for her losses and occasional victories, but she wasn't about to risk her neck.

'You can't be coming in here. I'll call my manager, Johnny. He won't put up with this.'

'We both know your errand boy's not here. I seen him leave earlier.' Des waved the knife in the air. 'I want what I'm fucken owed.'

Viola remained calm. 'All right, then. How much is it? Let me settle for Else.'

'I'll take whatever the house is holding, and,' he lunged at her with the knife, nicking Viola on the cheek, just below an eye. 'And I'll take whatever else I fancy.'

★

Gabriel had left the schoolyard immediately after first bell. He ran through the streets to Viola's and picked up his lunchbox from the kitchen table. He was about to leave the house when he heard a shout from one of the front rooms. He walked through the kitchen, along the hallway, and stopped at Viola's bedroom door. He hesitated before opening it. He saw Viola on her bed, laying on her stomach, with her face turned to the wall. Her dressing gown was hitched up around her shoulders, exposing her naked body. He saw a man standing by the bed with a knife in his hand. Gabriel turned to run and fell. The man leaped across the room and grabbed him by the neck before he could get to his feet. Gabriel was thrown across the room and slammed against the side of the bed. Mahoney bent forward to be sure Gabriel got a look at his knife.

'And who are you, darling?' he asked, in an almost gentle voice.

Gabriel was too terrified to speak.

Mahoney used the blade to lift Gabriel's fringe from his face. He whistled, a low cat-call, and rested a hand on Gabriel's thigh, lightly massaging it.

'Hey,' he said, quietly. 'Don't you be frightened, gorgeous. Viola and I are just talking.'

Gabriel had no idea what the man wanted but knew that Viola was in trouble. He began to cry and squeezed his eyes together. Mahoney tapped the boy on the chin to get his attention. 'I'm not here to hurt anyone, not today.'

Mahoney reached across the bed to where Viola lay, patted her on the hip and drew her dressing gown down. He picked up a diamond bracelet sitting on the bedside table and held it to the light. 'This will have to do for what Else owes me.'

He put the bracelet in his pocket, looking over at Gabriel. 'Hey, Viola. I'm coming back next week. Same time. You have one of your girls stay back for me. Unless you're willing to step up yourself.' He tousled Gabriel's hair. 'What a lovely looking thing. You do the right thing by me, Viola, if not I'll have to get in touch with the old Welfare molls. They'll fucking treasure this kid.' He gently stroked Gabriel's head. 'Either them or someone else will.'

The boy listened to the man's heavy footsteps walking back along the hallway. He waited until he heard the side door close and jumped onto Viola's bed. She reached out to him and started rocking him gently in her arms, kissing him on the forehead. She wiped the blood from her face and looked up at the ceiling.

When Viola heard Johnny return to the house she called him into her room. It had taken her precious little time to realise what she had to do. Gabriel lay in her bed, sleeping peacefully. Johnny could see the bruise across one eye and the fine cut below the other.

'Fuck! What's happened to you, Vee.'

'Nothing I'm about to talk to you about.'

'You will so,' he protested. 'Someone's hurt you. Who the fuck done this?'

Viola took Johnny's hand in hers, the only show of affection she'd provided him in twenty-five years.

'Listen, Johnny. There's something important I need you to do. You can't afford to get it wrong.' She squeezed his hand. 'So, will you listen? Please?'

Johnny wasn't able to listen. He was full of rage. 'Fuck this. You've been given a belt and I need to know who by.'

She gripped his hand. 'Shut up!' She pointed to her bruised eye. 'Do you reckon somebody would do this to me if they thought I had a hard man running the house with me? It's not what you do, Johnny, and never has been.'

Johnny dropped his head in shame.

She squeezed his hand a second time. 'Hey, it's not your fault. I never employed you to be a heavy. You're better than that. Police are supposed to look after me. I pay them enough, but they've grown fat and lazy on handouts. I need to be able to rely on you. Can I do that?'

'Yes, Vee. Of course you can.'

She reached into her dressing gown pocket and handed Johnny an envelope.

'There's more than enough cash there. Book a hotel room in the city for me. A couple of nights should be enough. The Australia Hotel. There's no sticky noses or riff-raff. Then I want you to organise for my stuff – clothes, perfumes, anything personal – to be packed up in boxes.'

Gabriel sighed and rolled from his side onto his stomach. Viola went over to the bed and sat with him.

'The boy's things as well.'

'And what will I do with them?' Johnny asked.

'Telephone Bobby Featherstone, the removalist, and pay him to move the boxes. Have him hold them until I've resettled me and the boy. I'll be in touch with you when the time comes to deliver everything.'

'Resettled? Are you going somewhere?'

Viola ignored the question and handed Johnny a bunch of keys. 'These are for the doors, the money safe and the liquor cabinet.'

'What am I supposed to do with them?'

'Whatever you like. The house is yours, starting tomorrow. You can run it however you want to.'

'I can't run this place on my own.'

'Of course you can. You've been here long enough, you know the business as well as I do. Even better than me when it comes to organisation. Besides, the girls love you, Johnny. You've never once laid a finger on any of them the whole time you've worked here. They trust you.'

'But what about you? You're running away from someone. I know it. I can't believe you'd do that.'

Viola sat back. She felt beaten and worn out. 'Don't you be judging me. I've had enough. I'm too old to take on another battle.'

Gabriel moaned. Viola moved across the bed, held his body to hers and cradled him until the boy settled.

'I need you to get him out of here tonight. Can you take him to your place until tomorrow morning and I'll come by and pick him up?'

'Sure. The wife will fall in love with him.'

'Good. And there's one last thing I need you to do.'

'Whatever you ask, Vee.'

'You find Frank Slim for me. Tell him I have a job that needs doing in a hurry.'

★

Around midnight Viola walked through the backyard of a dingy boarding house and into the kitchen. An elderly man sat at a table reading a foreign language newspaper. Viola recognised his face, having occasionally seen the man coming out of one of the local gambling clubs.

'Des Mahoney?' she asked. 'We need his room. Now.'

The man pointed above his head. 'Is here.'

She climbed the stairs, walked to the door at the end of the landing and turned to the man accompanying her. She nodded. He stepped in front of her and opened the door. The room stunk of cigarette smoke and piss. A kerosene lamp was burning on a table under a window, and empty beer bottles lined the mantle above a blocked fireplace. One wall of the room was covered with pictures of naked women. They'd been torn from magazines. Another wall was papered with clothing catalogue images of girls, some teenagers, others much younger. Mahoney lay asleep on his bed, nursing an empty bottle. He was covered with a grubby sheet. Viola walked over to the bed and shook him.

'It's wake-up time, Desmond.'

He didn't move. She shook him more vigorously, stepped back and waited. Mahoney slowly opened one eye, then the other, and looked up. 'What the fuck?'

'I've come to introduce you to somebody, Des.'

Frank Slim stepped out of Viola's shadow. He wore a black suit and tie and sported a crew cut. His dark skin was lined with fine wrinkles, uncommon for a man who never seemed to worry. Des sat up. He was naked. Mahoney knew without having to ask that the man standing alongside Viola could only be Frank Slim. He swallowed the lump in his throat.

'What do you want, Viola?' His voice quivered.

She answered by giving the slightest nod to Slim. He stepped forward and smashed Mahoney in the mouth with a closed fist, knocking his front teeth into his throat. A second punch broke his nose. Slim dragged Mahoney from the bed, knocked him to the floor and systematically kicked him on both sides of his rib cage, his back, arms and legs. Mahoney collapsed in front of the fireplace. Slim buried the heel of a boot into Mahoney's collarbone, dislocating it. Mahoney spat a mouthful of blood and several teeth onto the floor.

Viola raised a hand in the air and Slim stood back. She picked up the kerosene lamp. Mahoney's nose had shifted across his face. He looked up at Viola, spitting more blood.

'You fucking bitch. Cunts like you always need a man to do your dirty work.'

'I thought you were an ignorant bastard, Des. But you're so right. I do need a man,' Viola winked. 'What would you have a woman do after you've beaten her? Call the police? You know what I think, Des? If I were to get in touch with the coppers and tell them what you did to me, it might cost you as much as a round of drinks and a couple of cartons of cigarettes for them to forget the whole thing. Well, you can fuck that. What's happening right now in this shithole is my dirty work, delivered by my hired help. And guess what Des? I wonder if you know who will be paying? I'll give you a clue. It won't be me.'

'Get fucked, slut.'

Frank Slim waited for Viola to lower her hand. He moved

quickly. Neither Mahoney nor Viola saw the flick knife emerge from the sleeve of his suit pocket and slice a piece out of Mahoney's left ear. Before Des could scream out in pain, Slim swung a leg back and kicked Mahoney between the legs, expelling the air from his body. He gasped as the pain shot into his throat. Mahoney vomited, pissed himself and passed out.

Viola turned to Frank Slim. 'Wait downstairs.'

She sat down on a rickety wooden chair until Mahoney came to. When he eventually sat up his face was unrecognisable. Blood ran from his ear, down the side of his neck and onto his chest. Viola spoke calmly.

'You're not to go near my house again, Des. Not ever. You're not to so much as brush by another woman in the street. You see one of my girls, any girl for that matter, out and about, you cross the road. You fail to do that and he'll be back here to pay you a more intimate visit. You understand me?'

Although Mahoney was in too much pain to reply, Viola was satisfied he'd got the message.

'And, Des. My bracelet?'

Mahoney pointed to his pants, lying on the floor. Viola went through the pockets and retrieved it. 'Thank you, Des.' She placed the bracelet around her wrist and admired it.

'On second thoughts, if I were you, I'd invest in insurance. Like moving. Interstate would be my suggestion.' She opened the door. 'I won't be seeing you again, Des. You take care of yourself and stay out of trouble.'

She walked back downstairs into the kitchen. The old man looked up at her, anxiously. She knew there was no need to bribe or threaten him to ensure he'd keep his mouth shut. Viola liked the newly arrived migrants from Europe. They worked hard, were polite to her girls when they visited the brothel, and best of all, they had an inherent quality for minding their own business.

'You married?' she asked him.

'No. My wife is dead. A daughter, I have.'

Viola took the diamond bracelet from her wrist and handed it to him. 'Be sure she gets this for her next birthday.'

Frank Slim was standing in the laneway. Viola took two envelopes from her handbag and handed the first one to him.

'That's for the work tonight. Two as we agreed.' She then handed him the second envelope. 'There's double in there. Four thousand. You hear of Mahoney misbehaving in future, pissing in the street, public littering, whatever it is, you be sure it's the last sin he commits. You need any more than that, you contact me through Johnny Circio.'

Frank took the envelope and felt its weight.

'I do trust you,' Viola added. 'The men I know that have any integrity, I can count on one hand with a couple of fingers to spare. You're one of them, Frank Slim.'

She kissed him on the cheek and closed her handbag. 'I've scraped the shit from these streets off my shoes for the last time. I've a child to take care of.'

RAVEN AND SONS

SOPHIE PICKED UP THE PARCEL AND HELD IT as delicately as if it were a piece of fine glass. It was about the size of a tub of butter and weighed as much. She turned the box over. The faded yellow paper was scuffed at the corners and the bow of string holding it in place was frayed at the ends. Sophie held the label attached to the bow between a finger and thumb. The name and date, written in longhand, was barely legible. *P. Foley – 22 July 1958.*

Mr Carver coughed to get her attention.

'When the family decided to sell the business following the death of Mrs Raven, the new company agreed to finance the restoration of remains wherever possible.'

Sophie retuned the parcel to the shelf, where it took its place amongst forty or so others, similar in size and shape, the more recent ones encased in styrofoam boxes.

'Some of these are almost fifty years old. How long are you required to keep them for?' she asked.

'By law, only one year, after which time we are able to dispose of them.'

Sophie raised her eyebrows. 'Only a year? Why are they still here?'

Mr Carver straightened his silk tie and frowned, slightly insulted.

'Because we are Raven and Sons. And we have been operating a funeral parlour from these premises for over a hundred years.' He said nothing more, as if his brief history lesson was explanation enough for why the dead gathered on the storeroom shelf had not yet been disposed of.

When Sophie had received an email asking her to take on the job of despatching burial ashes by tracking down the living relatives, she did wonder if one of her friends was playing a joke on her. The undertaker's name, *Raven and Sons*, could have been conjured by Edgar Allan Poe himself. Before responding to the request Sophie had searched online and found that not only was the business legitimate, it announced itself as the oldest funeral parlour in the city, a claim reinforced by the décor of the premises with its dark velvet curtains, deep-grained timbers and gold embossed signage.

Mr Carver, as Sophie would later discover from the gossiping receptionist, *Miss* Henson, had married into the business decades earlier.

'Beyond any legal requirement this firm has always abided by a moral and spiritual obligation to the dead. We would not think of disposing of human remains in a manner that sits poorly with the family. Unfortunately, now that the business has been sold, the building and chattels, which includes these poor souls, will become the property of the new owners in six months' time, unless we can reunite them with family.'

Mr Carver led Sophie through the preparation theatre, where she felt an uneasy chill, and along a corridor into a small office. He offered Sophie a chair, before sitting at the desk opposite. He opened a ledger and turned it towards her.

'This is only the first volume of many,' he told Sophie, placing a fingertip under an entry and running it across the page. 'We have the name of the deceased, the name and signature of the authority, most often a family member, their last known address and the cost of the funeral.'

'That's it?' Sophie asked.

'Yes. Is it enough?'

Sophie, a trained genealogist, had a decade of experience, her work primarily compiling family trees for clients interested in tracing their ancestry. She ran an eye down the page. 'Well, if the signatory is still at the address listed here, finding them will be no problem at all. But you said earlier that you've already written to people requesting that they collect the remains?'

'At the commencement of the financial year, every year, Miss Henson writes to the listed authority for whom we hold remains. Occasionally we hear back from people.'

'What do they say?'

'Some are bemused. Perhaps the daughter or grandchild of the original signatory, who, having inherited a family property discovers that they are also the custodian of a great aunt's ashes. Others ask that we dispose of the remains ourselves, which we do, in a dignified manner. And occasionally someone will call and admit, with some embarrassment, to having simply forgotten to collect the remains in the same manner they may have left a suit at the dry-cleaners.'

Mr Carver placed the palm of his hand on his chest and sighed. 'I do not expect that you will be able to successfully return each of our holdings, but I must be sure that every effort has been made to do so before I walk out of here for the final time.' He looked across to Sophie with genuine sincerity. 'Are you able to do that for me? Make every effort?'

'Yes of course. With the more recent entries it should be a fairly straightforward matter of contacting the signatory. It may be best doing that in person, either by telephone or a home visit.' Sophie placed a hand on the ledger. 'May I?'

'Of course.'

She picked it up and flicked through the pages as she explained her approach. 'But with the older entries, it is possible the original signatory may have moved or passed away. In that case, I'll begin with some research at the registry office – Births, Deaths and Marriages – to try and locate the next of kin.' She patted Mr Carver on the back of his hand, surprising them both. 'You'd be amazed how easy it is to find some people these days. Most people have a Facebook page, even my own gran.'

Mr Carver turned up his nose. 'Facebook. People seem to have forgotten the virtue of humility.' He stared up at the pressed metal ceiling. 'I've been with the family for over forty years. Most people believe it is a morbid trade but it's nothing of the sort.' He stood up and offered Sophie his hand. 'In the short time that you will be with us, I hope you discover it to be an experience of great dignity.'

Sophie left the funeral parlour expecting nothing of the sort. She did not disrespect the dead, but nor did she hold them in reverence. She'd pored over many records of life and death in her work, some quite tragic. She was driven by a commitment to historical accuracy, not emotion.

Sophie enjoyed the new work. She began with the most recent funerals and found that in most instances the relatives had, as Mr Carver indicated, simply forgotten to collect the labelled ashes, finding themselves too busy to visit the funeral parlour. The remains were often those of an elderly relative who had lived alone and was widowed. Most of the cases were dealt with over the telephone, where it was agreed that the ashes would be collected. In some instances, families reneged on the arrangement and the ashes remained on the shelf waiting to be collected. As a matter of urgency, it was decided that the ashes would be sent to the next of kin by registered mail.

'Is this legal, sending the ashes through the post?' Sophie asked Miss Henson over morning tea, following a conversation she'd had with the youngest son of an eighty-five-year-old woman, who'd been awaiting collection for over two years. He'd moved interstate, to the far north–west coast. Sophie had managed to track him down through the family lawyer.

'He's too busy to come down this way and is happy for us to send her through the mail. Is that allowed?'

'It is perfectly legal,' Miss Henson explained. 'Although it has never been a regular practice of Raven and Sons,' she added. 'Until now. Mr Carver made this decison as a matter of necessity.'

'Why not?' Sophie asked. 'Until now?'

'When cremations were first introduced, the postal system was used to return the remains to family, particularly to those living in rural areas.'

Sophie waited patiently for Miss Henson to continue, as a means of explaining the apparent contradiction. But Miss Henson did not go on. As was her habit, she appeared to drift off, turning her head from left to right, as if mysteriously searching for a voice calling her name.

'But not Raven's?' Sophie prompted her.

'We did.'

'We did?'

'Briefly, until a terrible situation arose. The remains of a Mr Arnold Winter were posted to his wife, who lived out on a farm in the northern hills. Several months later we had a phone call from Mrs Winter, the man's wife, enquiring after her husband's ashes, which she claimed she had never received. It was established that the remains had in fact been delivered, but unfortunately to the wrong address.'

'How could that be?' Sophie asked. 'Surely no one would want the ashes of a dead person who they didn't know.'

'Indeed. What occurred in this instance was that the ashes were delivered to another Mrs Winter in the same district. A Mrs Winter who had also lost her husband. A most peculiar coincidence. The ashes were lost forever.'

The more explanation Miss Henson provided, the more confused Sophie became. She leaned across the desk in an effort to gain Miss Henson's full attention.

'Lost? When it was discovered that the ashes had been

mistakenly sent to Mrs Winter number two, did somebody attempt to retrieve them?'

'Of course we did!' Miss Henson appeared offended. 'Old Mr Raven made the trip himself. But it was too late.'

Miss Henson fell silent again.

'Too late?' Sophie asked. 'How could it be too late?'

'When Mr Raven arrived at the property and explained the situation, the second Mrs Winter finally understood why she had been sent two parcels and not one.

'How do you mean?'

'Well, her husband's ashes arrived about a week after his funeral, then a few days later a second parcel arrived. Our parcel.' Recalling the incident from decades earlier Miss Henson's face flushed with anger. 'The ridiculous woman had concluded that her husband had been sent back to her in separate lots. *He was a big man*, she told Mr Raven.'

Sophie still didn't quite get it. 'But how were they lost? The ashes. She could have handed them back to Mr Raven that day. Surely?'

'Surely not. When Mr Raven asked where Mr Winter was, *our* Mr Winter, the woman invited him onto the patio.'

'The patio?'

'Yes. The patio.' Miss Henson looked so distressed that Sophie wondered if she would be able to go on.

'And?'

'On the patio Mrs Winter pointed to a pair of sculptures. *Crude examples*, as relayed to Mrs Raven by her husband.'

'Of?'

'Of rabbits. The family had a deep affection for rabbits,

apparently. Also, Mrs Winter was an *amateur* artist. She claimed that on his death bed her husband had requested that following his death his ashes be mixed into the potter's clay that his wife used for her art, and that she sculpt him into an animal of her choosing.'

While Sophie's face showed little expression, she was thinking of ways to excuse herself from the room so that she could burst into laughter.

'And she chose a rabbit?'

'One that she fashioned the very same day her husband's ashes were returned to her, and a second rabbit when the remains of our Mr Winter later showed up. You can imagine how Mrs Raven felt when Mr Raven returned with a plaster rabbit under one arm and explained that it was Mr Winter.'

Sophie held the back of her hand to her mouth. 'Did you send him on to *our* Mrs Winter?'

'She wouldn't hear of it. Mrs Raven explained what had occurred over the telephone, and offered to personally drive the rabbit ... I mean Mr Winter ... to her home. Mrs Winter hung up on her and the next week we received a letter from Mrs Winter's lawyer threatening to sue. A cheque for one thousand dollars was posted to her by the end of the month.'

'And the rabbit?' Sophie asked as she stood; ready to run from the room.

'We did the only proper thing, of course.'

'And what was that?'

'We held a dignified service and buried him. Naturally.'

*

By the time that Sophie's six-month contract was up, the shelf of the dead had thinned dramatically. She had managed to locate either a family member or close friend willing to claim the ashes or grant permission for them to be disposed of. Each time she entered the storeroom Sophie would pick up the parcel she had held that first morning with Mr Carver. She had done all she could to locate the family, without success. The signing authority listed in the original ledger entry was a Mr Marcus Foley, aged forty-seven. Through research conducted in the registry office, Sophie discovered that Marcus Foley was the father of a child, Peter Marcus Foley, who died a little over a week after birth, in July 1958. Both the father and Mrs Lisa Dawn Foley, the child's mother, had since passed away. Sophie did further research of the electoral rolls and contacted an old friend from her university days, Max, who worked in the state probate office. Looking for a next of kin, Sophie asked him to check the register of wills and public trustee, with no success. As each parcel disappeared from the shelf, *P. Foley* appeared more alone and abandoned.

On her final day at Raven and Sons, Sophie once again went into the storeroom, picked up *P. Foley* and nursed him in her arms. Sophie took pride in her professionalism and efficiency. It annoyed her greatly that she had not been able to return the ashes of the newborn. But more than that, and to her own surprise, Sophie realised that she had formed an attachment to the deceased baby and was overwhelmed with a sense of responsibility towards his remains. As she was about to return the parcel to its place on the shelf, Sophie noticed something stuck in a fold of the paper. She released the fold. A fossilised earwig fell into the palm of her hand. She examined it closely.

Even in death the insect had somehow remained perfectly formed. Sophie returned the embalmed corpse to its tomb and placed the remains on the shelf. On her way out of the office that afternoon, Sophie made a sudden decision. Before leaving Raven and Sons for the last time she returned to the storeroom and placed the ashes of *P. Foley* in her handbag.

As her final job, that afternoon, Sophie drove across the river to the eastern suburbs. She had an address written on a piece of paper, the directions programmed into her mobile phone, and her handbag resting on the passenger seat. Forty minutes later she arrived in a street of neat post-war bungalows, with flowered gardens and modern cars parked in the driveways. While the houses were aged, young families were out on their lawns, walking dogs, their children riding bicycles. Sophie stopped outside number one-seventeen and got out of the car. The driveway was empty. She walked to the front door and rang the bell, several times. She felt so uncharacteristically anxious that she was relieved when no one answered. As she turned to leave she noticed an elderly woman looking at her from over the fence of the house next door. Sophie smiled at the woman and started to walk past her but changed her mind.

'Excuse me,' she began. 'Do you know the people who live here?'

'Not really,' the woman shrugged. 'It's a rental property. They've been here for three years, maybe. A young couple. I say hello, but that's about it. They're away. They are most weekends.'

'Actually, I was looking for people who lived here some time ago,' Sophie said. 'How long have you been here?'

'We built the place. Myself and my late husband, Eric. Sixty years ago.'

'Do you remember anyone by the name of Foley.'

The woman's eyes lit up. 'Of course. Lisa. Her and Marcus, they did the same as us. Their house went up a couple of years after ours. In those days the newspapers called us suburban pioneers.'

'And when did they move out?'

'Oh,' the woman's voice dropped. 'They were here four … no … just on five years. And then …' Her voice trailed off.

'They lost a child. I know,' Sophie said.

'Yes. Yes. Poor Lisa. She tried to put it behind her. But couldn't. Then one day, without notice, they were gone. A furniture van was parked here one day and the For Sale sign went up the next. She didn't even say goodbye. It upset me at the time. I didn't understand what she must have been going through until my own son was born.' The old woman made the sign of the cross above her heart. 'And I don't want to imagine what it would be like.'

'Do you know where they went to?'

'No. I never saw them again. Or heard from them.' She looked at Sophie more closely. 'Are you family?'

'No. No. It's a legal matter.'

The woman turned away, deciding that the matter was none of her business.

Sophie returned to her genealogical work, constructing family trees from the flimsiest of emotional connections but she could not forget about *P. Foley*. Each morning before she left the house Sophie would look across to the box of ashes on the bookshelf above the television, sitting where she had left them next to a maidenhair fern. She would contemplate ways of how she could return the ashes to the new owner of Raven and Sons without having to explain how she had come by them in the first place. She once called the funeral parlour to speak with Mr Carver and was surprised when the telephone was answered by a stranger who informed her that both Mr Carver and Miss Henson were no longer with the business.

'Where did they go?' Sophie asked.

'Into a retirement home, if they were lucky,' the voice chuckled. 'What an ancient pair.'

Late one night Sophie was asleep on the couch with a rug over her knees when she was woken by her mobile phone. It was her old friend, Max.

'Hey, Soph. Did I wake you?'

'You did. But I'm glad. Otherwise I'd have woken up in the morning not knowing where I was.'

'Maybe you need a man to get you into bed early?'

'It's why I don't have one. So I can go to bed when I like. What did you call for Max, other than to proposition me? Which you could do at a more decent hour, by the way.'

'You remember that name you asked me to chase up before Christmas? It was Foley. P. Foley.'

Sophie glanced across the room to the ashes. 'Sure I do. Why?'

'Well, I found him.'

She sat up. 'Found him? You sure?'

'I am. Unless it's a remarkable coincidence. I have the details of a Mr P. Foley, born on the twenty-second of July, nineteen fifty-eight.'

'Well, yeah. That's the same name and date. But you said mister.'

'That's right. I'd done an initial word search and nothing came up. Over the last month we've been in the process of decommissioning the old card index. By law, we have to cross-reference before they can be destroyed and I was sent a list of names that had missed the e-transfer. Your man Foley was on it.'

'But it makes no sense, Max. I was dealing with a week-old baby who died, not an adult. Can't be the same person.'

'Hmmm. Well, sorry to wake you, Soph. I thought it might be of help. Let's catch up for lunch soon.'

'Sure, sure. Hey, Max, why did you have this guy's details?'

'He was the administrator of a trust for his mother after his father died and she went into a home.'

'Do you have an address?'

The inner-city terrace was two storeys with a metal lace verandah, the kind of home Sophie sometimes dreamed of having for herself. She parked across the street and waited in her car, listening to the radio and watching the house. Just before dark, a man walked along the street, stopped at the front gate and checked the mailbox. To Sophie's eyes he could be in his mid-fifties. He was slim, balding and fit looking.

The man went into the house and closed the door. It took Sophie five minutes to pluck up enough courage to knock at the door herself. She could hear footsteps padding along a hallway. She was surprised when a young woman, barely in her twenties, answered the door.

'Hello,' the girl smiled, as if Sophie was an old family friend.

'Excuse me,' Sophie said, awkwardly. 'I'm after a Mr Foley.'

'Mr Foley?' the girl laughed. 'Dad. Sure. Come in.'

The girl ushered Sophie along a hallway of polished wooden boards, through a kitchen and into a lounge room overlooking a neat cottage garden.

'Wait here. He's upstairs. I'll call him. Who should I say you are?'

'Sophie.'

'Sophie? Okay.'

The girl went back into the hall and called up the stairway. 'Dad! Dad! Sophie's here for you.'

A few minutes later Sophie heard footsteps descending the stairs. The man she had seen in the street appeared in the kitchen. He looked a little puzzled. 'Sophie?'

'Mr Foley? Peter Foley?'

'Sorry, who are you?'

'I'm here from, well, on behalf of our business.'

'And what business is that?'

'We're a funeral business.'

'A funeral business? I don't know what you told my daughter but I have no interest in talking to a salesperson. I don't want to be rude but ...'

'You are Peter Foley, born on the twenty-second of July, nineteen fifty-eight?'

'Well, that is my birthdate. Yes. How do you know that? And it's Paul, by the way.'

'Your parents were Lisa and Marcus?'

'Yes.' He looked suspiciously at Sophie. 'What's this about?'

Sophie opened her handbag and took out a photocopied page from the funeral parlour ledger. 'Please, let me show you.'

She placed the piece of paper on the kitchen bench and pointed to the entry that specified the remains, including the father's name and signature.

Paul Foley could make no sense of what he was reading.

'That is my father's signature. And yes, it is my name and birthdate. But it's a mistake. As you can see,' he ran a palm across his own heart. 'I'm alive.'

'I have something else.'

Sophie again reached into her bag and brought out the box of ashes. She placed it on the bench with the identification label. Paul Foley reached into his shirt pocket, brought out a pair of reading glasses and studied the faded ink on the label. He took a step back and stared at the parcel with genuine puzzlement and even a touch of fear. Sophie looked from the ashes to Paul and back again several times before the question came to her.

'Were you a twin, Paul?'

'No,' he answered. 'I'm an only child.'

'Are you sure?'

He didn't answer, but didn't look sure of himself at all. Sophie noticed that a crimson rash had broken out on his neck. Paul was clearly agitated. He went into the hallway, where he opened a cupboard and retrieved a leather case. Returning to the kicthen he placed the case on the bench, slowly opened it and brought out a pale blue baby suit. It was slightly worn and stained. The top button was missing.

'This was mine,' he whispered to Sophie.

He reached into the case again and delicately held a second baby suit in his hands. He laid it alongside the first suit. They were identical, except that the second suit was new. It had never been worn.

PAPER MOON

CAROL SAT IN A WINDOW SEAT ON THE BUS clutching an unopened box of Minties. Seated next to her, her mother fidgeted with her white gloves, slowly pulling the tip from each finger, removing it from her hand, before replacing it and repeating the process. Carol looked down at the toes of her scuffed leather school shoes. The night before the long ride to the hospital she'd been ordered to clean them. They'd been left on the windowsill in her bedroom. Before getting into bed Carol picked up the shoes, examined them, then replaced them on the windowsill and looked outside at the full moon sitting low in the sky. At one time she'd been fearful of a full moon. She would watch each night as it became fuller and heavier, convinced that eventually the moon would sink into the earth and not rise again. Her father had heard Carol crying one night and she'd told him about her fears. He attempted to reassure her that the moon was not about to disappear. Unable to convince her, he made a papier-mâché moon, painted it yellow, drew a smiling face on it and, using a length of fishing wire hung the moon above her bed. Looking up at *her* moon she'd listened as her father explained that as long as it remained full, the moon in the night sky outside her window would also be safe. She did not doubt her father at all, and slept peacefully from that night on, full moon or not.

The bus slowed and stopped at an intersection. A small dog sat alone on the street corner. It leaned forward, studied the rush of traffic and lifted its rear end from the kerb. A truck charged through the intersection. Carol closed her eyes, sure the dog was about to race into danger. It didn't. The dog patiently sat again and looked right, left and right, just as Carol had been taught to do in school. She slumped in her seat, relieved. The traffic lights changed to green, the bus moved forward and the dog skipped across the intersection, obviously pleased with itself. Carol turned to her mother whose gloved hands were clenched together. She smiled and nodded her head slightly, a gesture Carol knew well even though she was only ten years old. She undertsood that her mother was doing all she could to convince her daughter that they were going to be all right, while not convinced of it herself.

After a few more stops the only other passenger left on the bus was a woman who looked to be a few years older than Carol's mother. She sat directly across from them. Her generous head of hair was shock white and she carried a carton of cigarettes in one hand and a dressing gown in the other. Carol noticed that she remained perfectly still, staring at the empty seat in front of her. Carol looked to the woman's chest, expecting to see it rise and fall as she took a breath. It didn't move at all. She began to imagine that the woman was dead, and that when the bus reached the end of the line the woman would remain in her seat for the return trip. She might never leave the bus, Carol thought, conjuring her own version of Purgatory.

Carol knew all about Purgatory. She understood that Heaven was the home of saints and those fortunate to be free of sin. Hell was a straightforward matter. It was *hell*. From the age of five, when she'd first entered the high walls of Saint Anthony's, she'd been constantly reminded that Hell was a place of eternal suffering and pain, punishment for the sins committed during life. If Carol didn't love God, she certainly feared him. She also realised the extent of his power and cruelty in creating Limbo, a place where young babies, both pure and marked by the stain of original sin, drifted for eternity, never to be reunited with their mothers. It was Purgatory that held the girls' attention. With no clear guidelines about how many prayers would grant leave from Purgatory, all the students of Saint Anthony's could do was pray, and pray some more, in the hope of eventual salvation. In recent months Carol had been praying vigorously for her father.

The bus turned off the highway into the hospital forecourt. Carol pressed her face to the window and looked out at the fortified red-brick building. The Australian flag hung limply from a pole next to a wide stairway at the entrance. As the bus came to a halt, Carol's mother stood up and took her daughter by the hand. Stepping from the bus, Carol was surprised to see tall trees, wide stretches of rich grass and garden beds bursting with brightly coloured flowers. Walking towards the entrance she noticed a woman wearing a floral dress sitting on the stairs nursing a plastic doll. The woman's dress was hitched high around her thighs, exposing her underwear. Carol knew she should look away but was shocked by the sight of deep bruises and scratches on the woman's legs. Walking up the stairs, she brushed against the woman and looked down to see a bare patch on the back of her skull. It appeared to have been shaved.

The foyer of the hospital sparkled. The tiled chequerboard floors had been mirror polished and the stark white walls held the sunlight pouring in from high windows along a spacious corridor. Carol sniffed the air. The scent of disinfectant, familiar to her from the school toilets, tickled her nostrils. They passed several people sitting quietly outside open doorways. Her mother stopped at a lift and pressed the button. Carol heard a cough, turned, and noticed that the woman who had been sitting out the front had followed them inside and was now standing behind her. The woman shuffled closer, the soles of her shoes squeaking against the tiles. She lifted her arm and rested her hand on Carol's shoulder. Too afraid to move, Carol closed her eyes and held her breath. The doors opened and she rushed into the lift. The doors jarred, jumped and finally closed.

Carol's father was sitting on a wooden bench in the far corner of a gymnasium. He wore pyjamas, the top buttoned to the neck. The room was littered with exercise equipment – barbells, stationary bikes, a rowing machine and several large plastic balls. A young man wearing an open gown and floral boxer shorts skipped along one side of the room, skilfully dribbling a soccer ball. Carol's mother paused, released Carol's hand,

and straightened her dress. She gritted her teeth, smiled, and walked over to her husband. She kissed him on the forehead and touched the back of her gloved hand to his cheek. Carol studied her father's face closely as she approached. He was wearing a new hairstyle. The sides of his head were shaven and a fringe sat across his eyes. He looked up at Carol, fixed on her in a moment of recognition and turned quickly away, his cheeks flushed.

'Say hello to your father,' Carol's mother said, coaxing her forward. 'Look, Paul. I've brought Carol to see you.'

He focused on Carol a second time, smiled but said nothing.

'Come on, Carol,' her mother urged. 'Sit here by your father.' She tried clicking her fingers together. The gloved fingers silenced the action. 'She has some sweets for you, Paul.'

Carol was nervous. She placed the box of Minties in her father's lap. They fell. The three of them looked down to the floor. The young man dribbling the ball weaved it between Carol's left foot and the Minties. Carol picked up the packet and held them in front of her father.

'For you, Daddy,' she whispered.

He took them and picked at the cellophane wrapper of the packet, one hand shaking slightly. They sat together in silence, watching the young man lap the room. One of the other patients began to applaud. Carol's father handed the Minties back to her and brought his hands together as if he was about to applaud also. Instead, he crossed his arms over his heart and stuck a hand under each armpit. Carol's mother nervously jumped from the bench. 'Let's go outside. Come on, the three of us. The air is so still in here. I need to get some fresh air.'

Carol walked beside her father. Although he moved slowly, he didn't shuffle as badly as some of the other patients. He'd always enjoyed a walk, and although she often had trouble keeping up with him, Carol had always followed in his footsteps. The family lived near the river and early each morning before heading off to work, her father would leave the house by the back gate and follow a track down a steep hill to the riverbank. He would walk the track until he reached a second hill, which he would climb to the street above to buy the newspaper. Back home he would turn on the radio and listen to the morning news as he made a cup of tea for himself, and one for Carol's mother. He would take a cup of tea to his wife in bed and drink his own at the kitchen table, reading the paper.

When Carol was about five years old, she woke early and listened for her father getting out of bed. Determined to join him for his walk, she put on her dressing gown and slippers and marched into the kitchen.

'What are you doing up so early?' he asked. 'Come on. Back to bed.'

'No, Daddy. I want to go with you.'

He was putting on his jacket that hung on a hook behind the kitchen door. 'But I'm going along the river. It's too far for you to walk.'

She refused to listen, and shook her head from side to side. 'It's not far. I want to come with you.'

He leaned forward, until the pair were looking directly at each other, eye to eye. 'Can you keep up with me? I won't be able to carry you if you're tired.'

'I won't be tired.'

'And you can walk all the way?'

'All the way, Daddy.'

He pointed at her slippers. 'You can't wear those. Your mother will murder us both if you get them wet. Let's get your gumboots on and keep your feet dry and warm.'

The air outside was fresh. They walked down the lane towards the river, an earthy scent drifting up the hill. Carol could hear birdsong all around and searched the trees above. Along the path a choir of frogs croaked from one bank to the other. On their return Carol began to tire. She didn't say a word to her father, and skipped along trying to keep up with him. It wasn't until they were halfway up the hill that her legs finally surrendered. She stopped to gather her breath. Her father walked on, and for a moment Carol thought he was going to leave her behind. He stopped, turned and walked back down the hill, squatting alongside her.

'You know what happens now, honey?'

She wasn't sure, considering the order he'd given her in the kitchen. She shook her head. 'No, Daddy.'

He touched the end of her nose with the tip of his own finger. 'I think it must be piggyback time.'

Her father carried Carol on his back to the top of the hill and through the streets to their front gate. She rested her head in the middle of his back, feeling the air rise and fall in his lungs.

When Carol and her parents exited the lift on the ground floor her mother noticed a man standing in the foyer talking to a nurse. She placed a hand on Carol's shoulder. 'Honey, can you take Daddy out to the garden.' She opened her bag, took out her purse and handed Carol a two-dollar note. 'Buy a drink for both of you and wait for me by the cafe. There's a table and some chairs. I need to speak to your father's doctor.'

Carol's father looked at his wife but said nothing. Carol took his hand. 'Come on, Daddy. Let's go.'

She led him outside and through the garden to the cafe. Carol's father stopped on the path and anchored his slippered feet to the ground. She tugged gently at his hand. 'Mummy said to get you a drink.' She pointed in the direction of the cafe. 'We can sit down under the tree. Do you want an ice cream instead of a drink?'

Her father squeezed her hand. 'I want to go.'

Carol felt immediately embarrassed, assuming her father was telling her he needed to go to the toilet. She had no idea where the toilets were.

'I want to go,' he repeated. 'I want to go home.'

Carol didn't know what to say. She also wanted her father to come home. From the first night he'd been away, when her mother was unwilling or unable to explain where he'd gone to, Carol had prayed he would return to them. When her mother finally told her that her father was sick in the hospital, although she had been upset, she was also relieved. Her closest friend at school, Shirley Latimer, had gone through a similar experience with her father. He went into hospital for an operation and was back home within a week. When Carol's mother couldn't explain what her father's sickness was, or if he'd had an accident or an operation, Carol became anxious again. She confided in Shirley the next day at school.

'She won't say what's wrong with him.'

'I don't want to say so, Carol, but maybe he's not in the hospital. He could be a runaway and your mum doesn't want to talk about it,' Shirley offered. 'One of my uncles did that. He ran away with a lady who wasn't his wife. And he never came back to his children again.'

Carol couldn't believe that her father would run away. He fixed broken dolls for her. He stopped her worrying over the sinking moon. He talked to her about birds and trees and flowers. He made the world safe. That night Carol desperately needed certainty from her mother that her father had not abandoned them, and told her what Shirley had said at lunchtime.

'Of course he hasn't run off,' her mother said. 'Don't be silly. I told you. He is in hospital, sick.'

'What sort of sickness?' Carol asked. 'When will he be better?'

'Well, it's difficult to say, with the sickness he has ...'

Carol watched closely as her mother stopped mid-sentence and moved around the kitchen, nervously wiping the benches with a sponge. Carol thought again about what had been said to her in the schoolyard and wasn't convinced that her mother was telling her the truth.

'If Daddy is in hospital, will you take me to visit him?'

Her mother sighed with resignation and threw the sponge into the sink. She turned and leaned her weary body against the bench. 'Is that what you want?'

'Yes.'

'Very well then. Tomorrow you can come with me to the hospital.'

*

Carol coaxed her father to a nearby bench and sat next to him. A patient walking past, stopped and asked Carol if she'd seen his missing dog.

'I've lost him,' he explained. 'Tommy. He's this high,' he gestured with an open palm. Before Carol could answer the man had walked on to the cafe and was asking the same question to people sitting at the tables. Carol could not take her eyes off the man, who was repeating the question over and over. He appeared stuck in a place he would never be free of.

Carol looked across to her father, realising they had to escape. 'It's time to go, Daddy. If you like?'

'Where?'

'Home.'

She looked over her shoulder and saw her mother on the far side of the garden speaking with the doctor.

'Hey, Daddy, remember the walks we used to take along the river?'

He looked at her and nodded.

'Well, we have to walk quicker now, like you told me to do. At the river.'

She took his hand. They walked past the cafe, skirting under a row of silver birch trees. When they reached the bus stop they sat in the shelter and waited. Carol was desperate for her father to say something that made sense, to show her he wasn't sick, and that returning home was a good idea.

'Daddy, do you remember the walks to the river? The first time we went you said I was too small. But I wasn't.'

She waited for him to reply. He leaned his head to one side, as if he might be hard of hearing.

'I was wearing my slippers and you said to me that I had to put my boots on or Mummy would get angry with you and we would be in trouble.'

She waited. The bus pulled into the stop, the doors opened and passengers got off, each of them wearing a face of apprehension. The bus driver looked at Carol and smiled.

'We walked,' her father said, slowly but purposefully, raising one arm and tracing a journey in the air with his index finger. 'I didn't think you would make it. But you did. Up the hill. Almost.'

Carol was so overjoyed she laughed. 'And then you carried me on your back.'

He squinted, as if straining to remember. 'Yes,' he nodded. 'I carried you. On my back.'

Carol took her father's hand, hopped on the bus, handed the money her mother had given her to the driver and asked for two tickets. The driver looked her father up and down.

'Where are you taking him?' he asked.

'Home,' she answered, without hesitation. 'We're going home.'

'Home?'

Carol stepped forward. She could not have been closer to the driver without touching him.

'Two tickets please.'

The driver handed Carol a pair of tickets and some coins. He looked at his watch. 'Take a seat. We don't leave for another five minutes.'

The pair walked the empty aisle and sat on the back seat. Carol slipped her arm through her father's and held on tight. He looked anxiously out of the window. They waited.

THE GOOD HOWARD

I'D ALWAYS SLEPT WELL, UNTIL THE WEEKS and months after my fiftieth birthday. I'd wake during the night with my heart racing, aware that I'd been dreaming, although I could recall none of the details. Too embarrassed to confide in my wife I decided to talk to one of the other managers at the office, 'Fabulous' Phil Ryan. I quickly realised I'd made a mistake. Phil told me that I should keep a pen and pad near the bedside, so that when I woke I'd be able to document the dream before it vanished. 'You put down the details while they're fresh in your mind,' Phil explained. 'And the next morning you go over them, you know, dream interpretation, they call it. I read about it somewhere.'

'But I can't write it down,' I said, trying to explain my predicament. 'As soon as I realise I'm awake, the dream, well, it's already slipped away. There's nothing left to write. It's gone. My mind's a blank when I wake up.'

Phil looked at me suspiciously. 'Well, if it's gone, how do you know you've been dreaming? And the night sweats? Sounds more like an anxiety attack to me. You must be worried about something?' He put his feet up on the desk and laughed. 'Maybe it's a midlife crisis. Fuck, you've just turned fifty. We all go through it.'

He stood up and patted me roughly on the shoulder. 'Don't let it get to you. Chat up one of the office girls. A night out on the town, that's what you need. Chase down a piece of stray pussy and you'll soon get over your worries. The only dreams you'll be having then,' he winked at me, 'will be wet ones.'

Phil's advice, like most of what he said, offered no help, although one thing that he said stuck with me – *you must be worried about something.* I wouldn't have thought so, not until he posed the question. But maybe I was? After waking from the dream I had an overwhelming sense that something was very wrong, that something catastrophic was about to visit me. I just didn't know what. By the next morning, after having finally drifted back to sleep, my wife would need to shake me awake so I wouldn't be late for work. I tried to convince myself that everything would be fine. *It is only a dream.*

But things aren't fine, and they don't get better. They get worse. The sweating and the nightmares, or what I think *may* be nightmares, continue. I become exhausted and am barely able to sleep at all. Until the morning I meet Howard.

The night before I had gone to bed resigned that I may need professional help to deal with my anxiety and then for a reason I can't explain I sleep right through. When I wake up I feel fresh and relaxed. It feels like a good day. Today will be my day, I reassure myself in the shower. I have a quick breakfast, grab the car keys, and go to leave for work, but the car refuses to turn over. I look under the bonnet before realising that I've left the headlights on overnight. I go back into the house and tell my wife that I am catching the bus. She wants to call the RACV there and then, but I tell her not to worry. There's no hurry. She can ring them later in the morning. I am taking the bus, I tell her. She looks at me as if I'm crazy. She repeats that she can make the call for me. But I tell her no. Today it will be the bus.

Rather than walk to the end of our street and along the main road to the bus stop, a ten-minute walk, I cut through the lane behind the house to a reserve and follow the creek that cuts through the suburb. I walk on the bicycle path that meanders beneath a line of trees along the creek. It is a beautiful autumn morning, crisp and clear. I feel so happy that I begin to swing my briefcase in the air. I even consider whistling. And then I feel suddenly light-headed and pass out.

When I come to, I am lying on my back. I can feel the familiar dampness of my shirt against my skin. But it is no night sweat. I look up to a dappled blanket of sky. I try sitting up. I feel dizzy and a little nauseous so I rest my head back on the wet ground and turn on my side, vomiting bile onto the grass. A fluoro-suited cyclist passes me just as I am clumsily getting to my feet. She brakes, turns an arc off the side of the bike path and comes back to me.

'You okay? Can I help?'

I look up. The woman is young and pretty. She has straw pigtails protruding from her helmet. She looks like a Viking. *Viking Woman*, I think to myself. I feel as if I am a little drunk. I want to laugh at her and tell her she looks silly. But I don't, because I realise that I am the one who must look silly. The knees of my pants are covered in mud, and although I haven't noticed it yet, I have damp autumn leaves stuck to the back of my suit jacket.

'Thank you, but I'm fine. I just tripped over on that tree branch, there,' I explain.

I search the ground, attempting to locate something, *anything* that may have been the cause of my fall. Her eyes follow mine, combing the ground.

She asks me again if I am all right before locking her plastic slippers into the pedals and taking off. I brush myself down as best I can, retrieve my briefcase and decide that although I am still a little uneasy on my feet I will continue to the bus stop. But I haven't taken more than a couple of steps when I feel a second wave of giddiness. I rest against the nearest tree trunk to stop myself from falling again. It is then that I lucidly recall my mysterious dream for the first time.

In the dream I am in my house, which although eerily familiar is not *my* house. I am running from room to room, becoming increasingly frantic as I open and shut the doors. I get to the end of the hallway, which is like the hallway in my own house but much longer. I find an open door and am welcomed into the room by a soft yellow light. As I step over the threshold I see my mother standing in front of me. She is very old, looking just as she did in the weeks before her death. She is wearing the floral housecoat that became her uniform; the one we teased her about because she was never out of it during those final months.

The room she is standing in is not a room as such, but another endless corridor. The walls are lined with floor to ceiling shelves. Cluttered along them are hundreds, if not thousands, of the cheap ornaments my mother collected during her lifetime. I feel afraid, certain that I have seen a ghost. I then see myself, or my reflection at least, in an etched mirror on a shelf behind her. But it is not the image of a fifty-year-old man I see. In the mirror I am a boy of ten again, a head of blond hair and the soft unmarked face of my youth.

I turn away from the mirror, back to my mother. She has transformed herself. No longer a hunched eighty-five-year-old housebound pensioner, she is a vivacious thirty-something. I see that she is wearing a pair of red dancing shoes that she always favoured as a younger woman. Long after she stopped dancing she kept the red shoes in a box in the bottom of her wardrobe. When I cleared out her flat after the funeral, I took the shoes out of the box and held one in each hand, standing in her empty bedroom. I eventually threw them into a plastic garbage bag along with the rest of her clothes and dumped them in a charity bin.

As I continue to the bus stop I replay the dream again and again, desperately wanting to make sense of it. I make a mental note that I will write down the details as soon as I am on the bus. At the bus stop, as I check the timetable attached to the bus shelter, I hear a voice behind me.

'The 8.05. The 8.05. He is two minutes late. He always is. He will be here in … in around ninety seconds.'

I turn to see a man, maybe a little younger than myself, sitting on a low red-brick fence. He looks vaguely familiar.

Perhaps I've seen him at the local shopping centre? He has one of those old-fashioned haircuts that seem to have come out of the Great Depression; a razor sharp part down the centre of his head, a fringe flopping over his forehead, shaved back and sides. His clothing comes from a similar era, although it is not *aged* or worn. He is wearing a chequered shirt, buttoned to the neck, a brown hand-knitted cardigan with wooden buttons, grey pants and a pair of polished brown leather shoes. He points to the timetable. 'The 8.05. It will be here in ...' he looks down at his own watch, 'sixty seconds.'

I do not answer, and walk to the other end of the bus shelter.

He is correct about the delayed bus. Just as the minute passes it pulls into the kerb.

My travelling companion motions me onto the bus in front of him. I look for an empty seat, at a safe distance from the elderly passengers huddled together down the front and a group of raucous schoolkids bouncing across the back seat. As he follows me down the aisle several passengers greet him warmly.

'Good morning, Howard.'

'How are you today, Howard?'

'Lovely morning, isn't it, Howard?'

I take my seat. Although there are several other empty seats he sits down next to me. He turns around and waves to a couple of passengers before smiling at me and offering his hand. 'Good morning, I am Howard,' he says.

I look down at his open hand before tentatively offering my own, although I don't offer my name. Howard studies my face. 'You don't catch this bus. The 8.05. You don't catch the 8.05. What bus do you catch?'

I look straight ahead and answer without making eye contact. 'No, I don't catch the bus. Not usually.'

He reaches across the seat and picks something from the shoulder of my jacket. I back away. He shows me the leaf of Liquidambar, held delicately in his hand. As he twirls the leaf between his fingertips the light picks up its bruised colours.

I open my briefcase, take out a client file, close the case and put the file on top. I don't want to talk to Howard, or anyone else. I take my fountain pen from my suit coat pocket and try concentrating on the paperwork, but it is a pointless exercise as I continue to worry over the dream, quizzing myself as to what it could mean. I take my notepad from the briefcase and begin writing.

Howard leaves me to myself for several bus stops. When we pull up alongside the railway station, the schoolkids from the back seat get off the bus. I pray that Howard will get off, too. But he doesn't. He has settled in next to me. Some of the remaining passengers begin pointing to Howard and call out to him.

'That's not you, Howard. You're the good Howard. That's not you, over there.'

I look up. They are all smiling at Howard, even the bus driver. He smiles back at them and nudges my arm, pointing to something outside. 'That's not me. I'm the good Howard.'

I look out of the window but have no idea what he is talking about. He points again. 'Look, that's not me. That's not me. I'm the good Howard.'

I finally see what he's referring to. It is a faded piece of graffiti scrawled on the side wall of the railway station: HOWARD LIED – AND SOLD OUT ON REFUGEES.

I don't get it. Not at first, at least. But when I do, I laugh, to myself mostly, and just loud enough so that 'good Howard' hears me. He leans across and smiles.

As the bus is about to pull away the railway gates come down blocking the traffic. Several minutes after the train has passed by the gates have not lifted. The bells continue to ring. The gates are stuck. I rest my chin in my hand and place my forehead against the window. I feel myself drifting back into the dream and force myself to sit upright, desperate to stay awake.

Howard leans across the seat. 'Are you tired? You look tired.'

I try ignoring him but he won't be put off. 'You have to get your eight hours, your eight hours. Do you get your eight hours? You look tired.'

I look across at Howard, finally accepting that I am stuck with him. 'No, Howard, I don't usually get my eight hours. I did last night, funnily enough, but most of the time, no, I don't get a great night's sleep.'

He rocks in his seat. 'I do. Eight hours. Nine hours. Ten hours. Why don't you get yours?'

I look down at the notes that I have been scribbling then back to Howard. He is waiting for an answer. 'It's nothing. I have dreams. They wake me sometimes.'

He becomes inquisitive. 'Dreams? You have dreams? What are your dreams?'

I look at him, this total stranger, who is probably a little strange as well. I peer out of the bus to the graffiti. The traffic is not moving. The driver gets on the microphone and suggests that we may like to get off and take a detour via the next train. A few more passengers exit the bus. I can't follow them, as I have to go across town. So I stay. And so does Howard, who is waiting for my response. I give in to his persistence.

As I recount the details of the dream Howard hangs on every word. When I stop I feel that my story is unfinished, that I need to say something more, although I am not sure what. I shrug. 'I don't know what it means. One of my work colleagues, he tells me that dreams need to be interpreted. If we learn to understand our dreams, we come to understand ourselves. But I can't understand much of my dream. Not yet, anyway.'

Howard is quiet. I look down at the notepad thinking about my mother. I feel reasonably certain that the dream must have something to do with her death. On the day of her funeral I could not stop crying. I was surprised by my reaction, although I shouldn't have been. After all, she was my mother. But in the weeks before it was all over, when she had been quite ill and was in pain, I had rationalised that she had lived a relatively good and long life. That her death would bring her peace, as they say. I had stood at the graveside, my crying audible, a little embarrassed in front of the other mourners. My wife put an arm around my waist, attempting to console me, 'It's okay, it's okay.'

Afterwards, she commented again that it was all right to cry. 'You used to cry all the time when we were younger, at the movies, when Elsie had her paw caught in that rat trap down the back. You even cried when your football team lost that final by a point. Remember that? You were like a blubbering kid?'

*

Howard pulls at my sleeve to get my attention. 'Tell me about the end again, the end of the dream.'

'The end?'

'About your mother, and the red shoes.'

I tell him again, about seeing myself in the mirror as a child, and then looking at my mother, suddenly much younger, all dressed up for a night on the boards.

Howard screws his face up then looks down at his watch before replying. 'Your dream, I think it is about dancing. Your mum, she liked dancing?'

My mother loved dancing, when she was younger, at least. She and my father would go to the fifty-fifty dance every Sunday night at the Brunswick Town Hall. As I sat on the bus I could see them in the front room of my childhood home, ready to go out on the town. Him in a black suit with his hair slicked back, my mother in those shoes.

'It's the dancing. I think you need to go dancing.'

I look across to Howard, bemused. I've never been dancing. I can't, in fact, dance. Before I can respond Howard suddenly jumps up from his seat and walks to the front of the bus. The driver opens the door and Howard moves to the lower step. The few remaining passengers call out to him, 'Goodbye, Howard, see you tomorrow.'

I watch as he walks to the other side of the road and stands alongside the graffiti wall. The boom gates lift, which causes the elderly passengers at the front of the bus to cheer in childlike unison. As we take off I look over at the Good Howard. He waves a gentle goodbye to me.

★

192

I can't say for certain if it is meeting Howard that improves my sleeping and keeps the restless nights at bay, but from the night of the bus trip, I feel calmer and sleep better. And not just for one night, but every night. I also feel healthier generally, and for some reason, lighter on my feet. Several weekends later I am down in the back garden turning over the compost. My wife is up in the kitchen going through the newspapers. I can hear music drifting onto the patio but cannot recognise what it is. When I finish I return the shovel and pick to the shed and walk up to the house, thinking about a cup of tea. I leave my boots and socks at the back door. I am greeted by the wonderful voice of Ella Fitzgerald belting out her version of 'Mack the Knife'.

My wife is at the kitchen sink peeling vegetables. As I walk past her on my way to the bathroom she looks over her shoulder and smiles at me. I pause for a moment and look down at her hips as they sway to the beat. In the bathroom I stare into my unshaven and wrinkled face, the warm soapy water caressing my hands. As I look down into the ivory sink and closely inspect my hands I realise that my bare feet have been shuffling an awkward rhythm back and forth across the tiles.

That afternoon we dance across the kitchen floor and keep the dance going long into the night. The next morning, lying in bed, I think about Good Howard and my good fortune, in meeting him. The following morning I leave the car at home and head through the park to catch the 8.05.

COLOURS

MY GRANDFATHER TAUGHT ME ABOUT THE SKY. At night he would take me out walking in the paddocks behind the government house we lived in on the Reserve. He'd tell me to look up at the sky while he took a pouch of tobacco from his pocket and rolled a cigarette. Pop would stay quiet until he'd finished his smoke, a habit he stuck with long after the advertisements on TV warned that people who smoked were going to die. Only when he'd finished would Pop point one of his nicotine-stained fingers at the stars and tell me that a night would come sometime in the future when the stars would save me. He'd wave a hand in the air, smile at me and raise his eyebrows like some cheeky kid sharing a secret with a friend. But the secret was his alone, seeing as I didn't have a clue what Pop was on about.

The grog was banned on the Reserve back then, but Pop could always find a way to get hold of it. He loved the drink. *Too bloody much*, my mum used to say. *The fool has cooked his brain.* Most in my family were teetotallers. Some had jumped on the wagon needing the fear of the Old Testament for support. Not Pop. He never feared the drink or the Bible, but he knew the grog did him harm nonetheless. *This girl* he would sometimes say, particularly when he was on the charge, *I love her, but sometimes she doesn't love me.*

Mum was working on the egg line in those days and it was Pop's responsibility to keep an eye on me. He did a captain's job when he was sober, but when he'd had a day out with the drink he'd sometimes forget all about me and wouldn't bother eating himself. I'd get hungry and take off for the supermarket, thieving ice cream and sweet biscuits, or on a good day, a packet of lollies.

Pop was also up for a fight back then. He'd take on anyone ready to put their fists up. He'd fought in the carnival tents when he was young and was pretty good, they reckon. But with the drink taking him down for the count, he ended up ruined. He'd open his mouth in the pub, announcing himself like a prize fighter and end up getting belted around like an old dog. The police went after him some days and locked Pop up. They didn't mind giving him a whack either. He never should have been treated that way, no matter how much trouble he caused.

Police in our town were as crazy as any drunk and nobody expected better from them. Pop knew as much and was always telling me, *You see the Gunjis coming, you run like hell.* And I did. Anytime the police drove down our street, or came to the door, I'd race to the swamp by the speedway and hide until they took off, sometimes with Pop in the back of the van, kicking at the doors and swearing his head off. They'd put him in the cells for the night and he'd come home the next morning with blood under his nose and maybe a cut on the head, complaining *the fucken Gunjis done this.* Maybe they did. It was their way. But then Pop could have gotten into a fight on the way home, too. Like some said, he could *find himself a fight in an empty house.*

I got caught with a bucket of chocolate ice cream under my T-shirt at the supermarket one afternoon. The manager called the police and they called a social worker. The Welfare was about to stop me seeing Pop, which meant my mum would have to quit work to take care of me, or give me up. But then she died, with no warning. She had a bad heart from the day she was born with some type of fever. She was always catching her breath between smoking plenty of cigarettes. She had been walking down the road after work at the egg factory with one of her sisters, my auntie Beryl, when Mum said to her, out of nowhere, *We had good times when we were kids, didn't we?* Then she fell down in front of Auntie and was dead.

The only way Pop could make sense of what happened was to blame himself. At the funeral he kneeled on the ground, grabbed two fists of dirt and shovelled them into his mouth, near choking himself. Some in the family were sure he'd gone crazy and tried to stop him, but then his older brother, Uncle Ronnie, stepped up to the grave, put his hands in the air and called out, *Let him be with himself.*

Pop lay on his stomach, cried into the earth and screamed. He told the ground he was ashamed of all the drinking he'd done and was to blame for his youngest daughter dropping dead in the street. Ronnie kneeled down next to Pop and told him he wasn't to blame at all. The years of drinking were his own doing, for sure, but it hadn't made him responsible for my mother's sick heart. The doctor at the co-op who signed Mum's death certificate said her heart had been *broken in childhood* and no matter what anyone had done she'd have died anyway, sooner before later. Not a word of what the doctor or Ronnie said mattered to Pop. He made a decision to put the blame upon himself, which produced pain for him, but some good also. He gave up the drink that day and never went back to it.

Pop soon found a way to get himself into a different kind of trouble. He'd march around town telling everyone, blackfellas and whitefellas both, that the grog was sinful, and people had no choice but to stop drinking if they were to become *decent*. His old mates quickly got sick of his preaching and threw empty beer cans at him and told him to *Fuck off home* when they saw him walking along the footpath. A couple of famous drunks, Salt and Pepper, who liked to call themselves *a national reconciliation project*, sat out front of the post office on the bottle most days. They went as far as to throw half a flagon of wine at Pop one time. The bottle smashed at his feet, staining the footpath red. When the police came to sort out the trouble, Salt and Pepper explained that Pop had driven them crazy with one of his sermons.

Pop had lived on the church mission as a boy, and spent time out with the old men in the bush before and after. His newfound spiritual talk was a jumble of what he'd been taught back then and the Bible verses he picked up again after a fifty-year absence. He made no sense to most people, me included, but he could tell a good story and I never got tired of sitting by his feet listening to one. After he'd quit the grog the Welfare got off his back and I was given permission to spend time with him after school. He'd make us a cup of tea and we'd watch *I Dream of Jeannie* on the television.

'That woman there,' he'd say, 'she's very strong on the spiritual.'

I didn't miss an afternoon with him until the year he had a stroke. It stopped him from moving one side of his body. He couldn't walk too well and could no longer speak properly. Auntie Beryl wanted to take care of him at home but struggled to keep up with the cooking, feeding and washing as well as going to work, even with me helping out.

It was decided he'd need to go into the old people's home beside the irrigation road that ran west out of town. Pop didn't want to go and became so angry I reckon he would have taken to the drink again, only he couldn't hold a glass in his hand without dropping it. He was miserable the day we had to leave him there, but when I saw him the week after he was as happy as he'd been in a long time. Blackfellas, yellowfellas and whitefellas, men and women, lived at the Home together. I'd never seen such a mixed-up mob. They all got on like family, singing songs and playing cards, the old boys telling dirty jokes, and the women doing each other's hair.

Pop loved the Home. Nobody was bothered too much about his rambling sermons. They enjoyed his company, even if a lot of what he said came out backwards. I enjoyed visiting him so much I'd head over straight after school most afternoons. We'd sit together until his dinner arrived, then I'd walk the mile back to Auntie Beryl's for my own tea. Pop liked to take me by the hand, propping himself up with a walking stick, and lead me out to the garden. He talked slow and dribbled his words but I got used to it and could understand most of what he said. He told me about *constellations* and said that blackfellas all over the country had their own names for the stars and their own stories.

One night he whispered a *special story* to me, slow and sweet, while tracing the location of each star on the back of my hand. It was a story I could tell no one, he said. My own story.

'Not even other blackfellas?' I asked him.

'No one. It belongs to you now. Take care of it. There's nothing more important to you than to remember which star belongs to you in the story. Right up there is your map,' Pop said, pointing his stick into the sky.

When I left that night the stars followed me down the road and along the bush track to Auntie Beryl's front door. Later, I looked out of the window. They were all there, watching out for me. And I could hear Pop, whispering the story in my ear.

The next weekend I was sitting with Pop in the dayroom and told him I was sure he was right, the stars were keeping an eye out for me, just like he'd said they would. He smiled and shrugged like it was no surprise to him at all. We worked together all afternoon, making our own Aboriginal flag – black, yellow and red – from coloured paper. Others in the room were making their flags too. Families all together. By the time we'd finished the floor was covered with scraps of coloured paper. I collected them and filled both pockets of my jeans. Pop closed his eyes a couple of times while we were sitting together. He'd worn himself out and asked if he could go to bed. I tucked him into his cot and gave him a kiss on the cheek. Afterwards, heading home, I skipped down the middle of the road, feeling happy, looking up at the stars.

I was not far from Auntie's place when I seen the *Gunjis* speed by, two coppers in the front seat and one in the back. I heard the car brake, looked around, and saw the car doing a U-turn. I started to run, like Pop had taught me, but I wasn't fast enough. The police car pulled onto the side of the road and blocked my path. The driver got out and slammed the door. It was Camel. Everyone knew Camel, and no one, even the other police, had a good word to say about him.

'Looks like you're running from trouble,' he said, hitching his pants up. I kept my eyes off him, looking down at the dirt until he poked me in the chest, real hard, and barked in my ear. 'I'm talking to you, you half-caste cunt.'

The other copper from the front seat got out of the car. He was a big young fella I hadn't seen before. He smelled of the drink.

'You been charging up?' Camel asked me.

I shook my head. 'Nup. I've never done that.'

'Fucken liar,' he said. 'All of you drink, young and fucken old.' He grabbed me by the throat with a claw and shook me. 'Liar.'

I couldn't breathe and wanted to cry.

'We'll have to take him in,' the other copper said. 'The kid needs a lesson.'

Camel stopped shaking me, smiled and patted me on the cheek. 'Yeah, why not?' He put his arm over my shoulder. 'Let's head back to the station.'

He pushed me in the back seat next to the third copper, who was sleeping, his mouth open, a bottle of grog in his hand. He woke and blinked across the seat at me like I was a mystery. Camel looked in the rear-view mirror as he drove. 'This fella is our little mate. Don't be a miserable cunt, Murphy. Share a drink with the boy.'

Murphy grabbed me by the jaw with one hand and tried pouring the alcohol down my throat with the other. Some went into my mouth and I tried spitting it out. Some went over my front, and the rest in the copper's face. He got angry and punched me in the mouth. I could taste blood, mixed with the grog. Camel called him off and they let me be until we were back at the lock-up. They walked me through the front office, one copper on each arm, with Camel marching out front like he was leading a lynching. Another copper, a lady sitting behind a desk, saw the blood on my face and the grog stains on my T-shirt. She stood up and was about to say something when Camel gave her a *shut it* look. She backed away and sat down. Camel grabbed hold of the keys swinging from his belt and opened a cell door. An old fella was in there, one of Pop's mates, Corky, laying on the cement floor in his own vomit. Camel opened a second door. The cell was empty. He threw me inside.

'Tidy yourself up,' he screamed.

The cell had no windows, only a rubber mattress on the floor and a toilet in the corner. I walked over to take a piss but saw the toilet was blocked. Messages had been scribbled on the walls, some written in shit, marking who'd been there before me and which copper was a NO GOOD DOG. Corky was moaning in the next cell. I sat down on the mattress, sure that when they came back the coppers would give me a good kicking. Or kill me. Pop had once told me there would be no place worse to die than in a police cell. If that was ever to happen, he told me, everything – his heart, his body – would be taken away from him.

I was afraid and my body started to shake. It was then that Pop came to me and put a hand over my heart. He whispered the secret story in my ear one last time. As he spoke I began taking the pieces of scrap paper from my pockets, black, yellow and red. I chewed on each piece of paper, rolled it into a ball and stuck the dot to the wall. I had soon made a map of the sky. My own constellation. Pop's and mine.

I could hear Camel marching along the passageway towards the cell, followed by the others. The keys rang out like a broken school bell. I stood up and pressed my body to the wall, where *my* stars were dancing, where my story was waiting to be told.

Camel unlocked the door. He was shocked to find the cell empty. He picked up the mattress and threw it against a wall. The big young copper got himself so wound up that he stuck his head in the toilet bowl, searching for the escapee. Murphy thought it looked so funny he laughed, pushed the toilet button and flushed his mate's head. The pair began throwing punches. Camel ignored them. He had something more on his mind to deal with. He stood in the middle of the cell, scratched his head and said, 'Fuck me, the kid's vanished.'

WORSHIP

LOLA INSPECTED THE ROOM A FINAL TIME, about to leave for the supermarket with a list. It wasn't that Lola was particularly forgetful, just that she hadn't shopped for a baby in close to thirty years. She looked up at the clock, nervous that she was running late. The morning ceremony had taken more of her time than usual. It was the third glass that did it. She'd long forgotten the medical term associated with her need to worship a cheap unopened bottle of red wine. *Addictive association* or *cognitive association*. Something like that. Maybe. She didn't mind. The treatment worked, which was all that mattered. She had stood before the mantle in her pink dressing gown and matching slippers, focused on the wine as she commenced the morning ritual, envisioning herself picking up the bottle, unscrewing the lid and pouring herself a full glass. She watched as her doppelgänger downed the glass and poured a second drink. Lola had soon polished off the bottle. Some days she added a little excitement to the ritual by visualising herself smoking a cigarette, loud music coming from a speaker above the imaginary cocktail bar and a handsome half-drunk dance partner. With the ritual over, Lola showered and dressed, confident she'd get through another day without alcohol.

Lola had never been religious, but a woman she met at an AA meeting told her that the reason she hadn't had a drink for seven years was down to reciting five Hail Marys before she left the house each morning. 'I swear by them,' she'd claimed. Lola never had the time or patience for such a lengthy penance, but made a point of making the sign of the cross across her heart each time she closed the front gate and headed down the street, rationalising that it could not hurt her recovery.

She turned the corner, walked by a park, and stopped at a red light at the intersection. A couple, a young man and older woman, had set up home outside the old hardware store. The shop had closed down the year before. The windows had since been whitewashed over, the front doors secured with a chain and heavy lock. A makeshift notice taped to the door warned passers-by to KEEP OUT. The frontage was favoured by the homeless during winter as there was no shopkeeper around to move people on. It was also well situated. Three doors down a new cafe had opened up that served a dozen different coffees, exotic teas and pastries. Men with beards, neck tattoos and pedigree dogs frequented the cafe and felt better about themselves after dropping a few coins in the bowl of someone sleeping rough for the night.

Lola had once bought a box of nails from the old hardware store but when she took them home and opened the packet she discovered all the nail heads were missing.

'That's impossible,' the beanpole of a shop assistant said, scratching his head when she returned to the shop and handed the packet across the counter. 'Did you snip them off?' he asked. It was as stupid a question as Lola had heard.

'Why would I do that?' she answered. 'So I could come back here and get into an argument with you? Come on, kid. Just give me my money back and you keep the nails.'

The boy did as he was told. Lola could be formidable when she needed to be, conjuring *bad Lola* from the old days.

As she waited for the pedestrian light to turn green, Lola watched as the young homeless man, a broom in one hand and a pan in the other, swept scrap paper and cigarette butts from the footpath. A pair of single mattresses lay under the awning, a neatly folded blanket at the base of each. A large flat-screen television had been propped up against the shop window. The woman, reclined in a canvas chair, directed the young man chasing rubbish with his broom. She rolled up the sleeves of her grey windcheater and sat back to watch the morning traffic crawl by. She squinted an eye in Lola's direction as she crossed the street.

'Do you have a smoke on you, love?' the woman called.

Lola hadn't enjoyed a cigarette since the day she quit alcohol. Not sure which addiction might trigger the other, she'd given up on both simultaneously.

Lola stopped. 'Sorry. I don't smoke. Used to.'

'Me too,' the woman chuckled. 'Now and then.'

'Sorry,' Lola repeated. 'If I had one, I'd give it to you.'

Lola kept walking on to the supermarket. She collected a basket and stopped at the end of each aisle to check through her list. She ticked off the baby wipes with the stub of an eyebrow pencil she kept in her pocket and paused at the disposable nappies, shelf after shelf of them. The list her daughter had provided didn't specify either the brand or type of nappy. She settled on a twenty-four pack – *10 kilograms* +. She gathered a few items not on the list, including a packet of sweet biscuits, *Scotch Fingers.* Lola was about to leave the supermarket, a bag of shopping in each hand, when she stopped at the counter. A teenage girl with a nose ring and pink dyed hair smiled at her. The girl wore a name tag – *Astra.*

'Can I help you?' Astra asked.

'Yes. Some cigarettes please.'

'What brand will that be?'

Lola couldn't remember a brand name. It didn't help that cigarette advertising had been banned. Or that they were secured, like contraband, in locked cabinets behind the counter. She shrugged her shoulders. 'I don't know. Give me some of your regular cigarettes. Something that's popular.'

'You're not a smoker?'

'No. They're not for me,' Lola answered. 'I'm buying them for somebody else.'

Astra smiled. 'That's what the young kids say when they come in to buy cigarettes. They tell me they're for someone else. A grandmother mostly. A grandmother at home who can't get up here and buy her own. My nan would never have sent me down the street to buy smokes, even if she did smoke.' She rolled her eyes. 'Can you believe it?'

'Yeah, I can,' Lola said. 'Started smoking when I was twelve. Loved it.'

'Really?' Astra replied.

Lola didn't keep a wide social circle, but got out enough to know that anytime you made a comment to a person under eighteen they'd answer, *Really?*

'Yeah, really. It's shocking, isn't it? What can I say?'

Astra opened a cabinet door, brought out a packet of cigarettes and sat them on the counter.

'These are our most popular brand. Because they're the cheapest, to be honest.'

Lola looked down at the packet, plastered with bold warnings – *SMOKING KILLS* – and a picture of a pus-filled eyeball.

'I can see what attracts customers to the brand,' she said, handing Astra a twenty-dollar note. 'The choice of serious risk-takers.'

'Really?'

Lola put the cigarettes in her cardigan pocket and walked back along the street to the vacant shopfront. The old woman hadn't moved from her canvas chair but the young man, done with sweeping, had buried himself under a blanket and looked to be asleep. Lola stopped and offered the woman the cigarettes.

'Here you go.'

She reached out and took the packet from Lola. 'Thank you, love.' She frowned at the diseased eyeball and turned the packet over.

'Sorry,' Lola said, 'the news is no better on the other side.'

The homeless woman looked down at a picture of a swollen tongue riddled with sores. 'Do you mind if I take two? One for my son?'

'They're yours. The packet.'

The woman delicately removed the cellophane wrapper. The young man under the blanket groaned and rolled over.

'That there is Robbie,' she nodded. 'He's worn himself out, carrying all our gear. We had a shopping trolley, but it got stolen from us last night.'

'People will steal anything,' Lola observed. 'I once had a boyfriend who had his glass eye thieved from a glass of water sitting by the side of his bed. Either that, or he lost it at the pub.'

'Nothing surprises,' the woman agreed. She took a cigarette out of the packet, put it in her mouth and let it rest on her bottom lip, searching her pockets until she found a box of matches. She lit the cigarette and took a long, soothing draw.

'Can't remember the last time I was offered a full packet of cigarettes.' She held up a plastic food container, exhaling at the same time. 'You know what's in here?'

'No.'

'Japanese food. They call it sushi. Fresh last night. I'm not game to get into the stuff. Don't matter. Robbie loves it. I'm happy to settle for a couple of slices of toast and a cup of tea.' She reached into her pocket and brought out a bottle of pills, rattling it in her hands. 'Now, these are Vitamin C tablets. A lady came by last night, gave 'em to me and said, "Take one a day. They'll keep you from catching a cold out here." I wanted to ask why she didn't leave me a blanket instead. But who wants to be ungrateful? You take what you can get.'

She reached under her chair and picked up a picture frame. 'What do you reckon I'm going to do with this?' she laughed. 'Have my portrait taken?'

Lola looked at the empty frame. It looked as lonely as a stray animal.

'Oh, that feels good.' The woman coughed, taking another drag on the cigarette. 'You sure you won't have one?'

Lola shook her head. 'Don't tempt me. It would be a smoke, followed by a big drink. Next thing I'd be back on *the* merry-go-round.'

The woman knowingly raised her eyebrows. 'Oh, it's like that. Pills and all. I understand, been there myself.' She held up the cigarette. 'This is it for me. These days. The streets are no place for a woman who plays. Dangerous enough as it is.'

Her son stirred and the blanket fell onto the footpath. She got up from her chair, waddled across and neatly rearranged the blanket over him. She leaned forward and kissed him on the forehead.

'You know, I've had some ordinary jobs over the years. I worked on a goat farm one time. That was hard going. Have you ever been kicked by a goat?'

'Not that I can remember,' Lola said. 'Doesn't mean that I haven't been, of course. One day I went to bed in a motel in Sydney and woke up in a car in Ballarat. Anything can happen.'

'Well, let me tell you, it hurts. I did fruit-picking over a few summers. That was hard as well, out in the heat. But no work I've ever done is as tough as being out here. Robbie spends half the day chasing a meal for us. The rest, he's looking for a roof over our heads.'

'Where are you from?' Lola asked. 'Originally?'

'The other side of the river. Out east. Near the mountains. We had a house for a while. But Robbie owed a couple of debts, and our place was burnt down on us. We run out of options over there, and he came up with the idea to try our luck closer to the city.' She looked over at her son. 'Well, luck's gone missing. My other kids have had it with me. But not Robbie, he's a good boy. Sticks fat. You got kids?'

'I have. A daughter. And a granddaughter,' Lola added. 'I'm taking care of her today.'

'How old is she?'

Lola wasn't certain. 'Ten months, about.'

'Do you have her often?'

'No. Today's my first time. My daughter's had me on probation until now.'

The old woman smiled knowingly. 'Oh. It's like that?' She smiled. 'You'll make it, I reckon.'

'Ta. I'd better head off. Can't afford to give my daughter a reason to call it off.'

'Will you be back this way again?'

'Yeah, of course. I come up here most days.'

'Good. I'll put the kettle on.'

When she got home Lola put the shopping away and again inspected the flat. She flushed the clean water in the toilet, straightened a crease on the bedspread and picked up a solitary piece of fluff from the carpet. She felt satisfied with herself until she noticed the bottle of wine on the mantle. She picked it up and ran into the kitchen, opening and closing cupboard doors until settling on a shelf below the kitchen sink. She lay the bottle of wine on its side and covered it with an empty hot water bottle. She stood back to see if the wine was sufficiently hidden. Satisfied, she closed the door, sat at the kitchen table and beat her fingernails on the laminex.

When Lola's daughter arrived with the baby she brought along a written list of her own. *It's long*, Lola thought, looking down at the column of dot points her daughter had created, *a manual for taking care of grandchildren*. The list included instructions for meal time, snack time, sleeping time, plus a few do's and don'ts, including *fresh air* do, and *sweet biscuits* don't.

Lola wasn't sure how sweet a Scotch Finger was, but her granddaughter, Isabel, had happily devoured two of them before her afternoon sleep. Lola was pleased with herself. The day had gone smoothly, even though she'd misplaced the list several times. While Isabel slept she sat in the kitchen drinking a cup of tea, surprised by how familiar and comforting the scent of a baby was after so many years. She only became anxious a little later, when Isabel hadn't woken, half an hour after the written note instructed that she would. Lola headed for the kitchen, opened the cupboard under the sink, took out the bottle of red wine and returned it to its rightful place on the mantle.

'Come on, let's associate,' Lola ordered.

She stood back and watched herself take the top from the bottle, lift it above her head and pour the contents down her throat, not stopping until the bottle was empty. Within seconds Lola's shadow collapsed on the floor. She looked down at herself, a little shocked. She leaned forward and gave herself a decent shake.

'You'll have to sort this out on your own from now on,' she said aloud, 'I have work to do.'

Lola heard Isabel babbling in the cot and went to the baby. Isabel looked up at her grandmother cautiously, before smiling. Lola was pleased that the baby seemed to recognise her. She lifted Isabel from the cot, pulled the bedroom curtain aside and looked into the street. The sun was about to go down, the early evening outside her window looked cold and still.

'So, your mother says that you love the fresh air. Do you? Let's find out.'

Lola changed her granddaughter and carried her into the lounge, sitting her on a rug in front of the television.

'Have a look at *Judge Judy* while I sort out this contraption.'

Lola unfolded the baby sling her daughter had brought over, turning it upside-down and inside-out in an effort to sort out how it worked.

'Okay, I think I've got it,' she whispered to Isabel, looping it over her shoulders.

Searching through the baby bag, she found a red knitted beanie and quilted jacket. She slipped the jacket on Isabel, buttoned it and put the beanie on her head. She lifted the baby gently into the sling then struggled with her own woollen coat.

'Are you ready for *your* fresh air?' she asked. 'I could be too old for this, but let's see.'

Lola was about to leave the house when she looked over at the sofa, at a rug draped over the headrest. She folded the rug under her arm, left the house and walked to the end of the street. She quickly felt the weight of the baby spreading across her shoulders and back. She stopped at the corner opposite the old hardware store, a little weary. 'I don't know if this was a great idea, kid. Next time we'll ask for a pram.'

A yellow flashing light on the roof of a council maintenance truck lit up the shopfront. Workers were loading a mattress onto the back. Lola watched as they collected a canvas chair, plastic food containers, a new pair of leather boots and the flat-screen television. When they finished, one of the workers took to the footpath with a heavy broom, while another connected a water hose to a fire hydrant on the corner.

Isabel shifted in the sling. Lola opened the top button of her coat and Isabel's head popped up, her wide brown eyes lighting up the night. The worker turned the water on at the hydrant and began hosing the footpath, washing away the cigarette butts and food scraps. Once they'd finished, the crew hopped into their truck and drove off. Lola crossed the street and stood outside the shopfront. The footpath was as empty as it was clean. She noticed an elderly man walking along the street towards her, carrying his life in a plastic garbage bag. She sat the blanket in the shop doorway.

'We best get back,' she whispered to Isabel, 'or your mother will give me hell.'

On the way home Lola detoured through the park. As she passed by the basketball court in the middle of the park she watched two teenagers, a boy and a girl, playing a game of one-on-one under the bright lights. Steam rose from their bodies as they dribbled the ball and weaved around each other. Each time one of them landed a basket the pair would generously high-five each other before again competing for points. The girl, wearing the famous Jordan 23, dribbled the ball towards the key and glanced over at Lola and the baby. She shot a basket, stopped and waved. Lola waved back and walked on. She could feel the baby's lungs lift and fall. She closed her eyes and imagined the baby's heart beating against her own.

Turning into her street, Lola saw her daughter pacing the footpath.

'Mum,' she called. 'Where's Isabel?'

'In here.' Lola unbuttoned her coat as she walked towards her daughter. Isabel looked up at her mother and smiled.

'You're sweating, Mum. Is there something wrong with you?'

'Yeah. I'm about as fit as a politician with a fat arse. I'll get better at this. Don't you worry.'

Her daughter gently quizzed her as she put the key in the front door.

'Did she have her sleep?'

'Slept like a top,' she smiled.

'And no sugar?'

Not if you don't count the Scotch Fingers, Lola thought. 'Definitely not.'

They walked into the flat. Lola sat on the couch and her daughter helped her unhook the sling. She lifted Isabel out and the baby kicked her legs in the air as if she was riding a bicycle. Lola saw the look on her daughter's face shift from a smile to a dark grimace. She pointed to the unopened bottle on the mantle.

'Mum. What's this doing here? Explain yourself.'

'Oh that,' Lola smiled. 'Explaining that is easy.'

Her daughter picked up the bottle. 'You haven't opened it?'

'Not in two years. It's probably turned by now.'

'Why do you keep it?'

Lola took the bottle from her daughter, walked into the

kitchen, unscrewed the top and poured the wine down the sink. She then rinsed the bottle clean of alcohol. Lola looked down at her granddaughter, who'd managed to wriggle herself into the kitchen on her stomach. Lola held up the bottle. 'I think we'll keep this.'

'Why?' her daughter asked. 'It's empty.'

'No, it's not.' Lola smiled. 'It just looks that way.'

ACKNOWLEDGEMENTS

To Erin, Siobhan, Drew, Grace and Nina – you'll never live off the royalties, but you do get the unwavering love. To Sara, I can only ask the obvious question – with love – how do you put up with me and maintain sanity? I also want to thank my extended family and friends, who are always there for me. To my RHS Class of '69, what a vintage year we were. In particular, and with deep appreciation, Peter Andrews, I owe you an ocean. And finally, Isabel, Isabel … the words will not end, and not forgetting Archie, Charlie and Louis.

The author would also like to acknowledge the following publications where versions of these stories have appeared:

— 'The Ghost Train' in *Kenyon Review*, Volume XXXIX, Number 2, Ohio, 2017.

— 'Harmless Joe' in *Here I Stand – Stories that Speak for Freedom*, edited by Amnesty International, Walker Books, London, 2016.

— 'Death Star' in *Crime Scenes*, pp. 103-116, edited by Zane Lovitt, Spineless Wonders, Sydney, 2016.

— 'Joe Roberts' in *Australian Love Stories*, edited by Cate Kennedy, pp. 73-81, Inkerman & Blunt, Melbourne, 2014.

— 'The White Girl' appearing as 'Spirit in the Night' in *Review of Australian Fiction*, Volume 10, Issue 4, 2014.

— 'Party Lights' in *Review of Australian Fiction*, Volume 20, Issue 2, 2016.

— 'Liam' in *Overland*, Volume 225, pp. 17-24, Melbourne, 2016.

— 'The Good Howard' in *Heat,* No. 11: *Sheltered Lives,* pp. 205-213, Giramondo Publishing Company, Sydney, 2006.

THE WHITE GIRL
Tony Birch

'Odette, be sensible. Sissy cannot leave this town.' Shea threw his hands in the air. 'Listen to me, please, Odette. It's not as if your Sissy is a white girl.'

Odette Brown has lived her whole life on the fringes of a small country town. Raising her granddaughter Sissy on her own, Odette has managed to stay under the radar of the welfare authorities who are removing Aboriginal children from their communities. When the menacing Sergeant Lowe arrives in town, determined to fully enforce the law, any freedom that Odette and Sissy enjoy comes under grave threat. Odette must make an impossible choice to protect her family.

In *The White Girl*, Tony Birch has created memorable characters whose capacity for love and courage are a timely reminder of the endurance of the human spirit.

> '… it is a rare thing for a novel to tell a gripping story while also engaging more broadly with the continuing dispossession and violence that are our uneasy inheritance.' *The Saturday Paper*

> 'Tony Birch's new novel goes to the heart of black and white relations in Australia, and puts the voices of women front and centre.' *The Big Issue*

> 'Rich in humanity and purpose, and hope. *The White Girl* is worth your time and will reward you over and over again.' *Australian Book Review*

ISBN 978 0 7022 6305 7

DARK AS LAST NIGHT
Tony Birch

Dark as Last Night confirms, once again, that Tony Birch is a master of the short story. These exceptional stories capture the importance of human connection at pivotal moments in our lives, whether those occur because of the loss of a loved one or the uncertainties of childhood.

In this collection we witness a young girl struggling to protect her mother from her father's violence, two teenagers clumsily getting to know one another by way of a shared love of music, and a man mourning the death of his younger brother, while beset by memories and regrets from their shared past.

Throughout this powerful collection, Birch's concern for the humanity of those who are often marginalised or overlooked shines bright.

> 'Tony Birch's short stories are precious gems … The pages of *Dark as Last Night* capture the humanity, courage and humour of characters in the midst of life.' *The Guardian*

> 'Birch's clear eye for detail, as well as for darkness and quirk of character, shines through at every turn.' *Books+Publishing*

> '*Dark as Last Night* is a reminder of the lives that can be shared through the short story, and what a punch they pack when written well. In this stunning, timely collection Birch brings a softness to real and fictional spaces that is sorely needed right now.' *Readings*

ISBN 978 0 7022 6317 0